Copyright © 2016 by Nick C. Brady

This book is a work of fiction, References to real people, events, establishments, organizations, or locals are intended only to provide a sense of authenticity and are used to advance the fictional narrative. All other characters, and all incidents and dialogue, are drawn from the author's imagination and are not intended to be considered real or factual.

All rights reserved, including the right of reproduction in whole or in part in any form.

Printed in the United States of America

ISBN: 979-8-525-84154-3

www.nickcbrady.com

Acknowledgments

To God Be the Glory for blessing me with the gift of creativity and the tremendous opportunity to share it with the world.

I would also like to thank my parents Cherrenelle Brady and Otis Brantley, and all my family and friends for consistently supporting me and my goals. I do not take your love and kindness lightly and I truly appreciate it.

Love you all.

Nick C. Brady

To the memory of my grandmother, Georgia Parish.

Nick C. Brady
NIGHT GHOST

"Nick C. Brady has a gift for setting the scene, crafting characters, and creating suspense. Night Ghost reads like anything but a first novel as words connect and passages flow, making for a hypnotic experience. Brady gets it. He doesn't tell, but rather shows in a way that feels as much cinematic as it does literary."

—John Darryl Winston

"Brady's smoothly paced narration pulls readers into a spooky and engrossing story of adolescent adventure and intrigues."

—*The Prairies Book Review*

"It is a must have and read! The writing is phenomenal from beginning to end! I love the journey the author takes you on!"

—Nate Greene

"Aside from the twists and turns that kept me hooked to the storyline, I absolutely enjoyed all the characters and the ways that they developed as the story progressed."

—A Lynn Powers

Prologue

FRIDAY MORNING, 2:48 A.M.

*T*wo hands gripped the wheel firmly on each end as they steered the car down the road. Cruising by alone at night. The knuckles were badly bruised, looking as though they had been previously bleeding.

Ahead, through the front windshield, the headlights reflected on the road through the hazy mist. Back beyond the curb, hiding in the dense darkness were several houses along the block. He caught a glimpse of himself in the rear-view mirror, then threw the hood of his gray sweatshirt over his head.

The driver relaxed his hands a bit, and began tapping the wheel rhythmically. He guided the vehicle onto the next block where the houses ended and many trees leading to a wooded area stood in their place.

The green numbers on the old radio clock now read 2:50. After crossing two sets of train tracks, the driver made a sharp left turn off the road and onto a bumpy surface.

He then shut off his headlights and removed his foot from the accelerator. Allowing the vehicle to calmly roll into the gloomy, isolated woods.

CHAPTER 1

FRIDAY AFTERNOON, 2:58 P.M.

The rigid terror all began with a deafening blare of the fire alarm, shrieking throughout the building. Suellen Blanchard jumped in her seat and began looking around nervously along with her classmates. The biology teacher, Mrs. Rivers had momentarily left the room to return a video to another teacher.

"I don't think this is scheduled," a girl shouted from the other side of the room. Just when the students were about to rise up from their seats to exit the room, the alarm suddenly cut off.

"Attention Millwood Middle School," a female's voice over the intercom announced, "please disregard that alarm. Again please disregard that alarm. Thank you."

Suellen let out an annoyed sigh as she wrote away in her notebook, finishing an assignment. She moved back against her seat and stared up at the digital clock high on the wall. With her left hand, she wrote a little faster while shaking her knee. Trying to finish up within the last three minutes. Even with her classmates chatting loudly around her, she stayed focused until writing her last sentence. She then closed her notebook and crossed both arms on her desk, waiting to hear the final bell. The fire alarm sounded again, but quickly cut off.

There's always something wrong in this lame school, she thought, irritably, still missing those long days during summer break that went by quicker than it had seemed to arrive. The only real excursion they'd taken that summer was in late July when Suellen and her family visited some of their relatives down south.

As the final bell of the day rang, Suellen rose from her seat and looked in the basket underneath to make sure she had all her belongings. She then exited the room with her other classmates.

Throughout the long middle school hallways, locker doors slammed, and crowds of students laughed and shouted to each other. A seventh grade boy ran down the hall screaming at the top of his lungs. He did that everyday after school. It got on Suellen's nerves.

"Thank God I'll be graduating this school year and headed to high school," she sighed to herself. As she walked the hall, she spotted her little brother in the crowd talking with one of his friends as they exited their classroom.

Suellen reached her locker and began to turn the combination lock. She gave the locker handle a hard tug, then sighed when it didn't open. "Wrong number." She quickly started again and pulled her locker open. She dropped her textbook on the inside floor and turned to the long rectangular mirror attached to the locker door. She did a quick twirl in front of the mirror, making sure she didn't have anything on her pink-faded jeans and the long-sleeved beige blouse. Her black snow boots were pulled over the hem of her pants. Suellen was the type of person who wanted her clothing to be perfect, having nothing on it, no lint, no string sticking out, and no stains. It always drove her parents crazy when she would take so long getting dressed and making sure her outfit was perfect from head to toe.

Suellen's light brown skin was nice and soft. She has a tiny circular birthmark on her left cheek and her thick brown hair was shoulder length and in a half ponytail.

She placed the notebook she had been writing in on the top shelf and pulled out her red jacket and pink backpack. Observing herself in her smooth mirror, the reflections of her two close friends, Brandon Dowell and Sabrina Morrison, appeared from behind her.

"Hey B, hey Slim," Suellen greeted, closing her locker and facing the two. Slim's eyes are wide and pretty. Underneath her brown bandanna was her long black hair which had a few brown streaks that matched the shade of her long-sleeved blouse. Her blue jean pants had small blue flowers on both front pant legs. She had her jean jacket wrapped around her waist, the sleeves tied in a knot in the middle. Suellen and Slim were always mistaken for sisters. They both liked practically the same things and looked alike. Slim was just a bit more petite than Suellen.

Brandon was a bit shorter than most boys his age, yet was quite strapping and athletic in all sports. But his all-time favorite was running. He planned to join the varsity track team next year when they all moved on to high school. Everyone thought he was a cool guy. He was friends with nearly all the eighth graders at their school. His clothing for the day was baggy denim jeans and a plaid denim shirt with its sleeves rolled halfway up his arm. Brandon's dark sunglasses were folded down, placed over the top of his shirt. He also had on a belt buckle he wore nearly everyday that read: SO SLY. His ears stuck out further than most people's. And he also has a slight mustache growing in.

"This has been the best spirit week ever! But it went by way too fast if ask me," he said, his thumbs under his backpack straps.

"Yeah it did," Slim agreed, adjusting her backpack on her shoulders. "This was one of the few times in the whole school year we got to come and not see someone else wearing the same thing. Back to the dull uniform on Monday."

With her jacket on now, Suellen threw her school bag across her shoulder. "Okay I'm ready."

They strolled down the hall, nearing the double glass doors that led outside.

The hallways were now quiet. The only discernible noise was a few kids still inside talking amongst themselves. Most of the students had left already or were outside waiting for their rides or the next school bus to arrive.

"BRANDON!" a boy's voice shouted from down the hall.

Brandon turned and recognized another one of his friends. "What's up?"

Suellen turned around and saw Brandon was talking to Derrick Jeffers, a boy she had a crush on. He was standing a distance away from them.

"You going to the game tonight?" he asked loudly.

"You know I'm there D.J.," Brandon shouted back.

Derrick laughed then rushed around the right corner at the other end of the hallway.

Brandon turned back the other way and followed Suellen and Slim. "What about you girls? You going to the homecoming game tonight at the high school?"

"Sure am," Slim replied.

Suellen pulled a small book out her jacket pocket and carried it in her left hand. "Wouldn't miss it," Suellen responded as they pushed the door open and left the building.

***

Strolling down the sidewalk, the three discussed how they hoped for victory at the football game that night. The gray sky above sent down drizzles. The air was motionless, but chilly. Slim had unwrapped her jacket from around her waist and was now wearing it over her brown shirt.

As they walked down the block, Suellen wheeled around when someone snuck up from behind and grabbed the book she held. Standing there with the book in hand was her twelve-year-old brother Andre, cheesing at her in his black jean pants and gray hooded shirt. He is the spitting image of his sister, only he had a similar birthmark on his right cheek.

Andre had been on the honor roll since the first grade. Last year when he was a sixth grader, the elementary school wanted to promote him to the eighth grade, but his parents thought he'd feel out of place in a school filled with teenagers. So they passed up that opportunity, much to Suellen's gratitude. She'd feel too embarrassed if her kid brother was a grade ahead of her.

Just because Andre was intelligent, that didn't mean he wasn't an annoying little brother at times. Although he irritated her occasionally, Suellen still admired Andre for his intellect, but she'd never tell him that. She was also protective of Andre, even if most of the time he felt he didn't need her to look after him.

"I've heard of this book," Andre remarked, eyeing it carefully. "Christopher Paul Curtis is a real good writer."

"Yeah he is," Suellen agreed, grasping for the book. But Andre pulled it out of her reach. "It's for our English class. We'll be reading and discussing it all next week. Some of the kids in the class were heated at the teacher for giving us a book to read that was over two hundred pages, but Mrs. Coleman didn't care. She said it was well worth reading and that it would prepare us for college."

"I could probably check it out at the library. Finish it. And write a ten-page thesis on it before you even get to the second chapter," her brother bragged, laughing at his own joke.

"You probably could. But nobody asked you all that, showoff," Suellen said smiling.

After fanning through some of the pages, Andre handed the book back to his sister.

"Here it comes," Slim warned.

Suellen glanced up and saw Georgia Parish Cemetery. It was an old, fairly large graveyard that hadn't been used in decades. It sat alone on a small block overrun with uncut grass. The cemetery had a thin cobblestone path in the center that led to the old brick-made funeral home.

Staring at the decrepit building as they slowly passed, Suellen shook her head sympathetically. *It's a shame the place had to be neglected*, she thought observing the shattered windows and overgrown grass. Then she focused on the eerie looking trees, and the black pointy gate that bordered the secluded area, and quickly turned her eyes away.

Slim strolled along beside her, trying to ignore the building.

Only three bodies were buried there, two on the right side of the path and one on the left. The tombstones were almost hidden by the long grass. The three large trees within the cemetery were spread apart. One on each far side in the front and the other stood directly behind the funeral home. Although the trees were tall and still producing leaves, it was easily seen that they were dying. The bark on the deep rooted plants was starting to sever and branches would frequently break off.

Further down, past the tree that stood in back of the funeral home was a sloping hill that led down to a large ditch, crammed with trees. The ditch ended and slanted upward on the other side, leading to the sidewalk on the next street over.

"I hear that place has been abandoned since the 1950s," Andre stated.

"Then why are they keeping it up," asked Slim. "It's not exactly a national landmark."

"A creepy landmark is more fitting," Suellen muttered.

"I can't believe you two are so scared of an old cemetery," Andre said, mockingly.

Here we go again, Suellen thought, rolling her eyes. *I should've just kept my mouth shut.* Unlike Suellen and Slim, the two boys weren't intimidated or even bothered by the sight of the graveyard. But it always annoyed her when they would rant about how it made no sense to be afraid of the old cemetery.

"How many times are we going to go through this?" Slim shot back.

"Until one of you can answer the question," Brandon said, facing everyone while walking backwards. "Why are you girls so afraid of a lousy graveyard? I mean I know we've never been in there. But that's no reason to be paranoid. It's just an old building."

"We don't know, okay," Suellen blurted out, unable to think of a better reply.

"That's the frightening part about the place," Slim defended, "you don't know what could be in there waiting. Especially in a cemetery that's been abandoned for well over half a century. I try to forget we only live three blocks down from it."

Andre threw his head back in a heavy laughter. Brandon just shook his head, letting out a deep chuckle.

"Aw come on, let's get real here now," Andre stated. "What could possibly be in there that's so bad?"

The girls gave each other tentative glances, their straight faces seeking for an answer in the other.

I guess I can see their side of this, Suellen said to herself. *It's not like something could grab you and suck you in there forever. But still, I don't know what it is, but there's something not right about that place.*

"Well?" Brandon asked, derisively. He turned and began walking forward, still ahead of everyone.

"They know there's nothing in there," Andre answered, strolling along between the girls.

"Well Andre, you're so smart, you're probably right," said Slim. She patted him on the head twice as his sister giggled. "But as for me, I can go my whole life not knowing and be alright."

Andre grinned with a playful sigh.

Before passing the cemetery by, Brandon cut his steps short and stood at a halt, staring at the tree on the far end. Suellen, Slim, and Andre did the same.

"Has a sign always been on that tree?" Brandon asked out loud, not talking to anyone in particular.

"I've never seen it,' Slim replied.

Suellen's eyes met her brother's, and they both shook their heads.

Brandon took a step closer and began reading. "This is private property. No trespassing. Violators will be prosecuted to the fullest extent of the law."

"Well they don't have to worry about me going there anytime soon. Or ever, for that matter." Slim remarked.

"It's so stupid though," Brandon stated. "What if a relative wants to come in and put flowers on their loved ones grave?"

"I doubt that'll come up," Suellen told him. "Those tombstones look like they haven't been visited or even cared for in a while. I don't believe those people had family. Or if they did, they moved away."

"Yeah, I guess," Brandon said with compassion before proceeding down the walkway. The others followed right behind without another word.

As they neared the end of the block, they saw the crossing guard standing with her back turned by the curb. Feeling compelled, Suellen stared back at the building once more before they got too far off. She gasped when she spotted the shadowy outline of a person walking by inside the funeral home.

Someone's in there! She thought, promptly swerving her head forward. She then began to walk at a faster pace, passing everyone else by.

"Slow down, Su. What's the rush?" said Brandon as he, Andre, and Slim caught up with her.

Suellen just laughed and continued even faster.

"Oh, so it's a race you want," Brandon called from behind her. Before she could reply, he sprinted by her and down the pavement. Everyone else took off as well, laughing and enjoying themselves as they playfully raced on home.

CHAPTER 2

"MILLWOOD CARDINALS! MILLWOOD CARDINALS!" is what a crowd of excited fans were shouting during the final play of the homecoming game. The football field was located behind Millwood High School. Down on the field, one of the players of the Millwood Cardinals bolted like a rocket to reach the in zone. The crowd continued to cheer.

The two players of the opposite team who tried to tackle him didn't even come close. When he reached the end zone, the buzzer went off. Everyone on one side of the bleachers stood up and cheered for the victory of their football team.

The Millwood Cardinals scored 49 to the other teams 40. The whole crowd jumped up in triumph.

Suellen, Slim, and Brandon were at the top of the bleachers rooting as well. The player who made the last touchdown did back flips down the field.

The entire audience erupted with laughter. Stepping down to go home, Suellen and her two companions giggled and pointed at him.

***

"That was a great game," Slim called, placing her hat on her head as she, Suellen, and Brandon walked home later that night. They weren't alone though. Some of their classmates who attended the game were walking on the other side of the street.

A chilly, but silent wind arose, carrying a cluster of cold dead leaves over onto the sidewalk beneath their feet.

"Yeah," Brandon stated, "it started off a little rough, but they came back strong after halftime."

Suellen started to speak, but instead stopped in her tracks. Slim and Brandon, unaware of her pause, kept walking. They crushed down on the leaves that had blown their way.

Suellen chewed on her lower lip and stared down the gloomy block, listening. *I wish this block had streetlights on it*, she groused in her mind.

"What is it?" Slim asked, staring back at Suellen.

Brandon stopped along with his friends and called over to them. "What's wrong? What are you two doing?" His hands pressed inside the pockets of his leather jacket.

"I— I— I think I heard something," Suellen stammered, trying to listen to confirm her suspicions.

All was quiet and cool on this mid October night. Then laughter from a distance broke out.

The three friends gradually continued down the path as Georgia Parish Cemetery soon came into view. As they drew closer to the graveyard, another soft chuckle filled the air.

"Sounds like someone's in the graveyard. That's all," Brandon whispered.

"That's *all*?" Slim remarked. "You say it like it's no big deal!"

"So you're saying you wouldn't be caught dead in a cemetery huh?" Brandon said, chuckling.

Slim snickered, "Shut up boy. You know what I mean."

Suellen crept near the tall, rusty gates with her two friends right beside her. They spied on two tall figures, coming from around the abandoned funeral home and walking towards the front.

"What are those boys doing?" Suellen whispered. The shady figures then began sauntering towards the exit.

"I don't know. But they look like they're in high school," said Slim.

The two continued their bantering as they approached the gate, their appearance becoming clearer. One of the boys wore baggy shorts and a white wife-beater despite the coolness of the night. Firm, thick muscles lined his arms. The other had on dark sweatpants. His black long-sleeved shirt had some kind of logo on the front.

They remained oblivious to being spied on until reaching the gate. Although their faces stayed hidden in shadows cast by one of the trees in the cemetery, Suellen knew they were watching them.

"Is there something we can do for you?" asked the boy in the wife-beater.

"We were just wondering what you were doing in there. That's all." Suellen replied, staring past them and at the rundown building.

"Don't worry about it," the other boy said harshly. "But if you're that nosy, we weren't doing anything in there. Just decided to cut across this dumb old graveyard. Not trying to disturb the peace of no one up in there. They may come after us."

"Say what?" Slim asked in a baffled tone.

The two boys fell silent as their eyes stayed on Slim. Their faces still buried in shadows.

"You kids have heard the ghost story, right?" one of the boys asked.

"Nope, I haven't," said Suellen. She looked at Slim and Brandon, who shook their heads also.

Both teenagers faced one another, then burst into heavy laughter.

"Man, you kiddos are young," one of the boys said through his chuckling. He turned to his companion. "Should we tell them the story, do you think?"

"Hmmmm.... I don't know if they're ready. They still have Enfamil around their mouths. Or is that Similac?" They laughed again, shorter this time.

"Are you all superstitious?" the other boy asked.

"Why? Need help spelling the word?" Brandon cracked. Suellen and Slim pressed their lips together to hold in their laughter.

"Lame, kiddo," the boy's friend replied. "Don't make us embarrass you in front of your two girlfriends."

Brandon just laughed under his breath, shaking his head.

"So what's this story you were talking about?" Suellen asked.

"Okay.... okay," said the other boy in the muscle shirt, "you kids might be able to handle it."

Grabbing hold of the old rusted gate, he leaped over to the other side. His companion did the same. From somewhere off in the distance a dog barked repeatedly. One of the boys snickered and said, "Whenever you hear a dog barking at night, you always know some psycho's lurking about."

"We're not as dumb as you look, you know," Brandon retorted.

"Okay now, kiddo," replied the boy in the muscle shirt. He threw his hands up and playfully took a few steps back. "You may not be so lame after all."

"Yeah maybe," his friend agreed. "But you still lose some cool points for not knowing the ghost story. It's practically an urban legend around here. What rock have you been living under?"

"Well, let's hear it then," Brandon insisted.

"Alright, well the way we heard it, it all started back in the early 1950s. There was a creepy old homeless guy who was always seen around here at night. No one knew who he was or anything. He was just some old bum who crawled out at night, asking for spare change. Most people would just ignore him, and he'd always call them selfish for it. But one day, he said it to the wrong ones."

"What do you mean by that?" Slim asked, nervously twirling her hair with a finger.

The two boys watched her for a moment. One of them snickered and said, "I know you aren't scared already…. are you, Princess? We haven't even gotten to the bad part. You sure you kiddos can take it?"

"Of course," Brandon replied quickly. He moved one step closer to them.

The girls, standing side by side, nodded in unison. Suellen's eyes fell onto the old cemetery. The overgrown grass swayed back and forth in the gentle breeze. She quickly turned away, telling herself not to stare at it again.

"Fine, if you're sure," the boy in the wife beater said with a careless shrug. "Well, one night, these three so called 'tough guys' were walking by and the homeless guy asked for spare change, like he always did. They just laughed at him, called him a few choice words, and kept on going. But…. when he called them 'selfish'…. that's when things took a turn. They approached him, and beat him down. No mercy at all. And with three against one, poor guy didn't stand a chance. It's believed he was dead long before they set him on fire."

Slim gasped, and covered her mouth with her hand.

Suellen just shook her head and muttered solemnly, "That's terrible."

"Yeah, that is pretty messed up," said Brandon.

"The three that did it were never caught. They came from wealthy families. So even though there were witnesses, their crime was covered up. No arrest, no trial. I guess money can really make things happen. Or not happen. However you want to look at it, I guess. But the guy they killed was buried right.... down.... there," said the boy in the black shirt. He pointed to the one tombstone that stood on the side by itself.

"The way the story goes, he haunts—and kills— anyone who walks over his grave. As a way of getting revenge for being mistreated when he was alive."

Slim, still covering her mouth in shock, gazed at the tombstone, and took a retreating step.

Brandon glanced back at the girls, trying to decide if they believed it.

"Do you know what happened to the cemetery? Why it was shut down?" Suellen asked. She was skeptical about the story, but still unable to set her eyes on the old graveyard.

"I hear the owner was doing some real crooked stuff," said the teen in the muscle shirt. "But it eventually caught up to him and all his businesses were shut down. Right after the homeless guy was laid to rest here."

For a moment, no words were shared between the five. Then the two older teenagers broke the silence with wild cackling, as if watching their reactions was the funniest thing ever. One of them leaned on the other's shoulder to keep from falling.

"Why you all so quiet?" one boy asked, wiping his eyes.

"I think it was too much for their little juvenile minds to process," his friend answered.

Brandon shook his head. "You can't expect us to believe his grave has a curse on it. And how come it's never happened? I've never heard of anyone getting killed by some old ghost."

"How should we know?" one of the boys answered back. "Maybe no ones ever been bold enough to try it. But we're not about to take any chances."

Still snickering amongst themselves, the boys moseyed on past Suellen, Brandon, and Slim.

"And you can believe whatever you want," one of them remarked without looking back. "That's all up to you, little dude. Either way, we're not losing sleep over it."

"Sure won't," the second boy shouted back. "We're only the messengers. Just make sure you and your girlfriends make it home alright."

They crossed the street and travelled off down another block.

"Well, that was interesting," said Brandon, strolling over to the girls.

"It was something, that's for sure," Suellen stated. A heavy breeze rattled the old black fence that caged the cemetery. Suellen backed away and moved closer to her friends, brushing the hair off her face.

"Do you two believe it?" Slim asked, her arms tightly folded.

"I don't know," Suellen replied. "I'm leaning more towards no."

"It does sound pretty farfetched," Slim agreed.

"I believe some of it," Brandon admitted. "Like what happened to the homeless guy, and why this old place got shut down. That might be true. But that whole walking over his grave thing sounds like some lame campfire story."

"It could be true. I hope it's not. But I guess I'll never find out cause I have no plans on experimenting with it," Slim said. Without another word, she continued down the block at a fast pace with Suellen right behind her as the two started chatting, unaware that Brandon wasn't following.

He stayed behind and faced the cemetery, bathed in shadows. The decaying trees that stood on each side gave it a bleak appearance, as if it were haunted. Taking a step forward, he edged closer to the gate, and noticed a faint orange glow through the window. The light was so dim, he wasn't even sure if it was there. *What in the world is that?*

He jumped with panic in his heart at the sound of a crow calling out in the darkness.

Staring down the street, he spotted Suellen and Slim as they started onto the next block. With no hesitation, Brandon darted after them. But the ominous glow inside the funeral home remained.

joystick. *He's playing one of his car racing games*, she realized. *He'll never notice I'm gone.* She turned from Andre's room and started down the stairs.

The flight of stairs curved once to the left from the top. Suellen carefully slinked down one step at a time. A car drove by, bringing quick-moving light through the dark room. Her heartbeat quickened to a galloping throb. Her biggest fear at the time wasn't sneaking out and going to an abandoned cemetery after dark; it was getting *caught*.

She made her way to the bottom of the stairs when she stumbled over something on the floor. The sound of a creaking floorboard arose from the top of the stairs. Suellen swiftly steered her head upward with a gasp. *What was that? Is someone coming downstairs?* She quickly tried to think of a plausible excuse as to why she was dressed to go out just in case her dad or brother turned on the light.

Taking a deep breath, she gawked toward the dark hallway above her. And spotted no one.

Still hesitant to walk on, she waited to see if she heard the sound again. Aside from the remote snoring of her father, no other sound came afoot.

Continuing on, she reached the door, opened it, and stepped outside.

"I can't believe I'm doing this," Suellen murmured before closing the door and trotting off.

***

The full harvest moon in the dark blue sky didn't bring much light down to the murky block. And despite the chilly night air, Suellen swabbed sweat off her forehead with the sleeve of her coat. Leaving her front walkway, she travelled down the block.

It wasn't until after Suellen had successfully sneaked out that she realized how tense she was. *I don't think I've ever been so nervous*, she thought. Her shoelaces, having become un-tucked, danced wildly with each step. She bent down to tie them when she was immediately approached.

"Hey," Suellen glanced up and greeted Slim, who was dressed in blue jeans and a dark blue jean jacket. "Have any trouble creeping out?" Suellen asked as she stood back up.

"A little. Tonight of all nights my mom talks forever on the phone. She usually goes to bed pretty early. Especially when she has an early shift at the hospital the next day. But she finally went on to sleep. How about you? Any trouble?"

"Not so much. Andre was playing some video game in his room. And today was the first day of my dad's week off from work since July. So he was

CHAPTER 3

On Saturday afternoon, Suellen, Slim, and Brandon were hanging out at The Millwood Student Center, a local place kids could go to play games, do homework, and just have fun.

Most of the kids just called the place MSC. Suellen and Slim played a game of foosball. Back and forth the ball rolled across the table as they hit it with the rotating bars. Finally, the ball fell into a slot.

"One more and you win, Su," Brandon reported, sitting in a chair. "But when I play you, it's gone be a different outcome."

"You better be glad. 'Cause you sure can't beat me," Slim remarked. They all laughed.

The building was filled with kids and teens running around, having a good time. Three young boys were running from a little girl as they played tag. A young red-haired female worker soothingly told them to take it outside on the playground. The four kids went out the back door and continued their game.

Suellen glanced up from the game and saw her brother enter the building. He went over to the other side of the room.

"Point for Slim," Brandon called. Suellen got unfocused and missed the ball flying her way. She quickly retrieved it from the slot at the low end of the game table.

"Hey Su, have you heard from your mom in Mississippi yet?" Slim asked before taking a sip from her water bottle.

"She called yesterday morning after my grandmother picked her up. My granddad's supposed to have his kidney transplant next Friday. Wish we could've all went to be there with him. But my parents didn't want us missing too many days of school."

"I'm sure he'll be fine," said Slim. She set her water aside and gripped the rubber handle bars, ready to start again.

"Oh yeah, he definitely will," Brandon agreed.

While Suellen and Slim refocused on their game, Brandon remained seated. He threw the hood of his gray sweatshirt over his head, leaned in his chair, and sighed heavily. He looked off to the side, watching golden sunlight glisten through the rectangular window.

"Oh yeah, I almost forgot," Brandon stated, facing his friends again. "I saw the craziest thing last night when we were by that old funeral home."

"What?" Slim asked, not looking up from the game.

"Well I don't know what it was for sure, but it looked like a light shining through one of the windows."

Suellen scored another point, winning the game. "Are you serious?" she then asked.

"As a cardiac arrest. I don't know what it was, but it was weird."

Slim moved from the foosball table and sat in the chair next to Brandon. "I don't understand why they don't just demolish that old place," she said. "It's been abandoned for how long now? What good is it doing just sitting there rotting away?"

Brandon moved up in his seat and shrugged. "Like I said, I don't know. Don't really care. I would like to get a closer look at his headstone, though."

Suellen and Slim eyed him, their features twisted in confusion. "What for?" They asked in unison.

Brandon approached the foosball table. He removed the white ball from the slot, and began tossing it in the air repeatedly. "It's something new and different. Which is rare in this wack town."

Slim arched an eyebrow at Brandon, then shook her head. "I guess. But you can count me out."

"I'm with her," Suellen agreed. "But you can go, Brandon. Be sure to write us after you get locked up."

Over the intercom a man's voice announced for all the kids between the ages of five and eight to go to the gym. Dozens of young children ran in that direction, playfully pushing and shoving each other, filled with excitement and laughter. Once all the younger children were gone, a heavy serenity smothered the room.

Right down from the foosball table, a crowd of teenagers stood watching their peers play a game of pool. And at the other end of the room was Andre, competing in a game of air hockey with one of his friends.

"I know you all aren't worried about that stupid sign," Brandon sighed. He tossed the ball up one last time, and kept it in hand. "Nothing bad's going to happen. I just want to go look at the tombstone and leave. Plain and simple. You can at least tag along with me. You know, so I can have witnesses."

Suellen rolled her eyes over to Slim, and both girls grinned.

"You sure you're not just scared to go alone?" Slim teased. "I mean, you did see something pretty strange there the last time. Maybe it was the spirit of that homeless man warning you to stay away." The girls cracked up.

Brandon sighed, resting his palms on the tip of foosball table. "So you two don't care about me now," he said tragically. "What if something happens to your boy? What would you do without me?"

"Live on," Suellen remarked. All three of them laughed this time. Some of the teenagers by the pool table glanced over.

"You two do me so wrong," Brandon said through his laughter.

"Okay, I'll come with you," Slim decided.

"I guess I'm in too," said Suellen.

Brandon lowered his voice and said, "Then it's settled. We'll sneak out tonight and meet at the Georgia Parish Cemetery by midnight."

"Why can't we go in the daytime?" Slim asked.

"We have to go late so no one will see us and we won't get caught," Brandon replied. "You know the adults around here like to mind everybody's business but their own."

Brandon, imitating a game of basketball, gently threw the white ball as if he were scoring a point. It landed hard in the middle of the foosball table. "You ready to play, Su?"

"Sure am."

As the game began, a dreadful scenario began to stir in Suellen's mind. She was so unable to focus on the game, Brandon had already scored his first point. He went and retrieved the ball from the slot and tossed it back on the game table.

Maybe I shouldn't go through with it, Suellen thought, still distracted as she tried to keep up with the white ball being rolled and kicked about the foosball table. A deep insecurity had settled in her heart, making her rethink her agreement. Struck with sudden doubt, she started to wonder if something would go horribly wrong that night.

CHAPTER 4

Later that afternoon, Suellen sat in her living room on the cushioned seat by the window with her bare feet stretched out and her head pressed against the back wall. She found herself disengaged from the book she was reading for school. She folded it down on her jean-clad legs and stared out the window. The gray puffy clouds that overcast the sky threatened rain.

I hope Dad and Andre make it back in time, she thought.

Earlier when their father picked them up from The Student Center, he took Suellen home, then took Andre to the park so they could play football. Suellen was offered to join them, but she declined. If her mother was in town, they might have gone out somewhere too. Or just stayed home and chatted.

But since Suellen had the house to herself, her mind wandered off to Georgia Parish Cemetery. She had walked by it many times in the past. And although it made her a bit uneasy, she never allowed it to bother her too much. But after learning of the ghost story, she now wondered how true it was. And what other secrets might be dwelling in the abandoned cemetery.

I wonder if those boys made that whole story up. Cause I've definitely never heard it before. Never even heard anyone mention it.

She stared at the watch on her wrist. The time was 3:58. *Eight more hours to go*. She sighed, tapping the wall with her feet repeatedly as her legs trembled.

When she agreed to join in, it seemed so long ago. But now time was creeping up on her. And she still didn't feel like it was something they should do. There was just so much that could easily go wrong.

She drummed her fingers on the book spread across her legs, then quickly snatched it up and began reading again. Trying to remain focused would hopefully put her nerves to rest.

CHAPTER 5

The digital clock on Suellen's nightstand read 11:48 p.m. She stared at herself in her bathroom mirror above the sink, brushing her hair. In the house she and her family lived in, all the bedrooms had separate bathrooms. That was the main feature Suellen loved about her house.

She had thrown on her jeans, with a small brown trench coat over her shirt, and was nearly ready to walk out the door. For the last few hours she had been debating whether or not she should actually go. Even considered making up an excuse saying she had fallen asleep. But at the very last minute she chose to be noble and keep her word.

After stepping out the bathroom, Suellen went over to the closet door and did a quick twirl in front of the long mirror. She then strolled to her bed and sat to put her shoes on, still feeling in her heart that things wouldn't go as planned tonight.

Sneaking out and coming back in sounds easy. But so much could go wrong, Suellen thought.

The time had changed to 11:51. Suellen stuffed the laces inside her shoes and rushed over to the long mirror again. Once she brushed her loose hair a few more times, she strolled towards her bedroom door. Grabbing hold of the smooth marble doorknob, Suellen opened the door and stepped out.

Walking down the gloomy hall, she stopped at her parents' bedroom and saw the door was ajar. Peeking around the corner, she saw her father snoring peacefully as he lay alone in bed. Suellen then went down to her brother's room and heard him playing his video game, accelerating with the knocked out in bed. If the house was on fire, I still couldn't see him getting up."

Slim snickered. "I would hope he would, especially since he's the fire chief." She eyed her wristwatch. "It's five till midnight. Let's get on down there so we can get on back home."

They paced down two more blocks before the first glimpse of the burial ground came in sight.

The two friends crossed the street and walked along the sidewalk. Suellen reached the gate door first and searched for the handle. She felt around on the old dry black paint that had been peeling for a while now. It didn't take her long to see the handle on the gate had broken off and it could just be pushed open now.

But before her hand touched the corroded gate again, she paused, her hand beginning to tremble midair. She yanked her hand back at once, as though it had been burned. Her eyes roamed across the cemetery, watching the decrepit building as it sat in total darkness.

Suellen forced her eyes away and turned to Slim, who had placed her hands into her jacket pockets. She stood her head leaning back, her eyes closed.

"You're not the only one that's tired, Slim."

"Why does he even want to do this?" she asked, turning to look down the block.

Suellen shrugged. "Probably just for the thrill. You know he craves excitement twenty-four, seven."

Slim cracked a smile and shook her head. "Yeah he does."

As they stood by the curb, Suellen couldn't abandon her nerves. She could feel the building's dark glare, as if it were challenging them.

"He'd better hurry up or I'm gone," Slim said through a yawn. "I'm exhausted."

Suddenly, the rapid thud of sneakers hitting the pavement emerged. Soon, Brandon ran up to them wearing black jean pants with a matching sweatshirt. In his right hand was a red halogen flashlight.

"Took you long enough," Slim sighed.

"What?" Brandon remarked in mock innocence. He flaunted a smirk and said, "I wasn't that late." He went past the girls and pushed against the gate. The bottom of the gate scraped against the ground as it opened. Once observing the area, and seeing no one around, they entered the deserted graveyard.

"Okay, so there are only three graves here, so his can't be that hard to find," Brandon figured. Flicking the flashlight on, he began walking to the two tombstones that stood side by side.

The girls stayed behind and kept a close watch of their vicinity. Down the street in the direction they had come, blue headlights drew closer. The vehicle slowed, and made a right turn down another avenue, leaving the street empty, silent, and dark in both directions.

"So far so good," Suellen muttered.

"Pssssss, Slim, Su. I found it."

The girls looked over and saw Brandon had moved to the other side by the one headstone. They strolled through long grass, stepping over fallen brushwood until they reached the tombstone.

Brandon bent to his knees. The flashlight he held cast a bright arc of white light on the broad, crooked gravestone. With the gray headstone having a smooth and legible texture, its appearance looked almost new.

"This is it!" Brandon exclaimed in a hushed whisper. He held down the tall grass with his free hand.

Suellen and Slim lowered themselves to the ground to read the engraved inscription.

Robert Otis Caldwell
Sunrise, June 12, 1901,
Sunset, September 24, 1952.

The girls stood to their feet again.

"Guess they found out who he was," Slim remarked, rubbing her hands together. "It's still kind of sad though. He died because of foolish, ignorant people. Even if he was homeless, he was still a human being." She shook her head solemnly.

Suellen blew into her hands three times, and shoved them back into her coat pockets. She glanced up at the rundown building, then quickly averted her eyes. She couldn't deny the fact that the old graveyard never set well with her for some reason. Even before hearing about the ghost story. But here they were, alone at night, standing in the midst of the burial ground. Whether the story was true or not, Suellen knew she didn't want to be there any longer. She found herself wishing she had just stayed home.

Focusing on the gravestone again, Suellen ran her eyes across the words etched on it as she pondered, *I wonder how they found out his identity?*

Brandon stood up and stretched. He let out a long, refreshed moan, as if he'd just awakened from a good sleep.

"Okay we've seen his grave," Slim said, yawning. "Can we go now?"

Before anyone could answer, a group of birds scattered from the left broken window of the funeral home. Their wings flapped loudly as they flew off. Flaring the flashlight toward the creatures, Brandon leaned his body back. Slim and Suellen ducked low to the grass, eyes cast upward, watching the flock of birds as they fled the cemetery.

"Not a good sign," Slim declared as she and Suellen hoisted back to a stand.

"That was something I wasn't expecting," said Brandon, a little shaken.

"I really think we should get going now," Suellen demanded, breathing heavily.

"Alright, alright," Brandon replied. He shined the light back on the gravestone, then gasped. He jolted as a sudden noise drew his attention, and he began to survey the area. "What was that?"

A soft groan was the only reply. He directed the flashlight at the tree on the other side of the cemetery. A second low moan filled the air. Brandon kept the tree cast in the light, and soon revealed a headless body as it emerged from around it. With its arms outstretched, the figure began staggering towards them.

It let out yet another groan, this time louder as it slowly staggered closer.

CHAPTER 6

Suellen folded her arms and sighed wearily. She muttered to herself as she walked toward the figure, the tall grass brushing against her pant legs.

"What are you doing out here?" She demanded.

The beheaded body groaned again, but this time the groan ended in laughter. Suellen pulled down the gray sweatshirt it wore, revealing her brother's face. His wide grin contrasted with his sister's scowl.

He snickered. "Hey, Sis. Don't you know you're not supposed to wake a sleepwalker? You could've killed me."

"I could never be that lucky," she remarked, rolling her eyes.

Slim and Brandon came over to join them.

"You have fun following us out here?" asked Brandon.

Andre leaned forward in wild laughter, holding his stomach. "Sure did. One of my friends told me the story of that homeless guy who got murdered. And I heard you all talking about it earlier and about meeting out here tonight. Just couldn't help myself." He looked past them to the other side of the cemetery. "Is that his grave right there?" Without waiting for an answer, he jogged over towards it. Brandon followed behind.

Suellen faced Slim, who stood beside her silently watching the two tombstones down on the other side. Suellen started examining the headstones as well. Both monuments were so terribly damaged with rust and scratches, the imprinted words were unreadable.

"It's so weird, isn't it?" Suellen asked her friend. "I just don't understand how these tombstones can look so raggedy and the one over there looks almost new."

"I know. That's a little creepy," said Slim.

Suellen looked over and saw the boys talking softly to each other. The air was heavy with chill, and she tightly folded her arms. She started to feel a morsel of guilt about sneaking out, and suddenly couldn't wait for the night to be over.

"Hey Su, look at this," Slim whispered.

Pivoting her head, Suellen watched her friend as she gawked at the decrepit building. "What's up, Slim?"

"Look! Do you see it?" She pointed to the glassless window, then quickly brought her finger back down.

Suellen briefly looked in the direction, then turned back to Slim. "What is it?"

Slim took a step back and shook her head solemnly. "We need to leave now. I just saw someone in there."

Before Suellen could respond, she heard the faint voice of someone calling to her and Slim. She soon realized it was Brandon. He and Andre were hiding behind a tree, whispering out to the girls.

"Get over here before they see you!" said Brandon.

Veering their gazes down the street, the girls saw bright headlights in the near distance. As the vehicle edged closer, red lights began flashing on top of it.

Slim let out a short shriek as she and Suellen sprinted over to the boys by the tree.

I knew something would happen! Suellen thought, wishing she had stayed at home. She was more angry than terrified. *I got to make me some new friends! This boy's about to get us all arrested!*

Brandon peered around the trunk of the tree, spying on the police car as it continued down the road. "I think they're going to keep moving. They may not have seen us."

"They wouldn't turn their flashers on for nothing," said Andre.

"We have to get out of here now," Slim whispered. "We got other problems."

Andre twisted his face in confusion. "Say what?"

"Ssshhhh," Brandon ordered. His eyes followed the moving vehicle, praying it would keep going. But to his chagrin, the car slowed to a stop on the opposite side of the street. "They're coming out!"

Suellen bit her lower lip as her anger now shifted to fear.

"Come on," Brandon whispered. "We're going out the back way." He led the way as he and his companions ducked low, sneaking alongside of the funeral home towards the back.

"This is the police!" shouted a man. "We're ordering you to come from hiding now!"

"You're trespassing on private property!" a woman announced.

The front gate creaked open, scraping against the ground.

"They're coming in!" said Brandon. "Hurry up! This way!"

CHAPTER 7

Suellen looked back once, then twice. She took slow, calm breaths, trying to make as little noise as possible. Brandon guided them past the old building and to the sloping hill that led down to the ditch. In the dark, it looked like a bottomless gap in the earth. Examining it, Suellen saw that the grass hill sloped down much steeper than she originally imagined.

Andre shook his head. "No way we can get down there without—" He was cut short by creaking floorboards coming from inside the building behind them.

"If someone is in here, come out now," said the female officer. Sharing not another word, Brandon was first to start slowly working his way down. With a sigh, Suellen staggered down after him. Her steps were gradual, but her heartbeat was rapid. Gazing back, she saw her brother and Slim following them.

"We're ordering you to come from your hiding now!" the male officer repeated, closer this time.

Reaching about halfway down, Suellen and the other three half-ran as they frantically hurried down the grassy hill.

"Ahhh!" Brandon cried out when he lost his balance and tumbled downhill the rest of the way. He came to a stop in a rustle of parched leaves layered on top of the dead grass. Andre, Slim, and Suellen reached the ditch right after Brandon did.

"Hide!" said Brandon. He climbed to his feet and brushed leaves off his clothes. Each of them ran in separate directions and quickly hid behind the nearest tree they could get to. Suellen tripped over an upraised root, but landed silently behind the tree it belonged to. Initially, she made no attempt to get up. She covered her mouth with both hands and shut her eyes. Time seemed to move at a snail's pace. But she waited…. and waited…. and waited, all the time wondering if they should just take a chance and make a run for it. After listening for a while, and hearing nothing, she grew confident the police were not aware of their whereabouts, and she gradually rose to her feet. She slowed her heavy panting. Her breaths turning into mist in the air.

Peering around, Suellen spotted her brother hiding behind the tree in front of her. He relaxed his head on the rough tree bark and took a short breather.

"Where did Slim and Brandon go?" Suellen whispered.

A bright white light emerged from the top of the hill and waved across the ditch several times. Suellen looked off to the left, and caught sight of someone else hiding further down where the ditch met another grassy hill. The dark figure was crouched to the ground and didn't seem to notice Suellen staring directly at him. *That's got to be Brandon down there*, she assumed.

From the top of the hill, the two officers exchanged a few words before sauntering off in the distance, leaving the ditch in the gloom.

Suellen leaned her back against the tree and sighed out of relief.

"Close call," Slim said, leaves crunching beneath her shoes as she stepped beside her friend.

"This is too much excitement for one night," Suellen remarked.

"But it does keep you on your toes," Brandon stated. Suellen turned and saw him and her brother walking alongside.

"You made sure not to get caught hiding all the way on the other side Brandon," she told him, pointing down the ditch.

Brandon turned to the direction she pointed, then back at Suellen. "I wasn't down there at all. Slim and I weren't too far from your brother. Over there." He tilted his head to the opposite direction.

Suellen looked to where she had before, only now the figure squatting by the tree was gone. "But…. I saw someone. I thought it was…." She rubbed her side as her stomach began to cramp with uneasiness.

Maybe, she thought, *we were better off going with the police instead of running from them.*

"You saw someone down here?" Andre asked her, roaming his eyes across the area.

"I saw someone too," said Slim. "Right before those cops came. Someone was walking around inside that old building. All I could see was a shadow, but I know someone was in there."

Brandon stared off for a moment, then turned his head up toward the funeral home. "It's time for us to go."

With no objections, they rushed down to the opposite end and cautiously started scaling the grassy hill. Once reaching the top near a street light that stood high above them, they continued down the sidewalk, marching in silence.

The orange light nearly lit up the whole block. As they walked, their dark shadows reflected ahead of them on the pavement. Suellen was the only one to stop and spy back down at the dark ditch. Her hands began to perspire at the thought of someone else being down there with them.

I guess this old cemetery isn't completely abandoned, she thought, feeling her socks go damp with more sweat. *Someone's definitely still here. Even Brandon saw something strange the other night.* She gazed down at the many trees, searching through the wooded area. *Maybe it was....* Suellen silenced that notion and took a brief moment to reinforce her belief that ghosts didn't exist.

But beneath her assurance, the unspeakable word still lingered.

Forget it. I'm gone. Suellen managed to break away from her morbid thoughts.

She shivered, zipped up her jacket, and hurried down the pavement to catch up.

CHAPTER 8

After running most of the way back, they slowed their pace as they reached the next block. Most of the houses sat in darkness. But Suellen was only focused on hers and began walking faster towards it. She and the others stopped once reaching her front pathway.

"Well…. this has been some night," Brandon said.

"Yeah, a night I'll really try my hardest to forget about," Slim muttered, pulling out a leaf tangled in her hair. She strolled closer to the curb and prepared to cross the street to her home. "See you all later, if we don't get caught sneaking back in, that is."

Suellen grinned a little. "Okay, bye."

Andre and Brandon gave her a short wave before she jogged across to the other side of the block.

"Alright, well peace out, you two," said Brandon as he stared at his house further down. "Lost that flashlight I brought. Would go back and get it, but I'm not that big a fool."

"Could've fooled me," Andre remarked.

Brandon snickered. "I'm too tired to clown with you, little man. Later." He turned and continued down the pavement, walking with a strut.

He's such a guy, Suellen thought, rolling her eyes. She and her brother then rushed to their front door.

"I only locked the bottom one when I left out," Andre informed her, approaching the door first and pulling out his keys.

Suellen rubbed her hands together. "Then hurry up before Dad wakes." She looked over her shoulder and glanced down the dark street, feeling somehow watched. Her eyes moved across the houses on the other side of the street, searching for someone in the windows, but seeing no one.

With the twist of a wrist, Andre promptly unlocked the door and pushed it open. After their entrance, Suellen silently shut and secured the door. She wasn't sure if it was out of impulse or fear. With her body pressed against the door, she closed one eye and stared with the other out the peephole, her heart beating swiftly along the wood.

"What are you doing?" asked her brother from the stairway.

"Just making sure the police didn't follow us back or anything," she told him, beginning to make her way through the darkness toward the stairs.

"No way. They didn't see us," Andre whispered, remembering their father was asleep.

Hope they're not the only ones who didn't see us, Suellen said to herself.

She had made it halfway up the stairs when three slow knocks emerged through the house. They both froze and gawked down to the gloomy living room.

"Someone's at the back door," Andre said under his breath. He spun his head about, looking up the stairs, praying to himself that their father hadn't heard and wasn't on his way down this instant.

Suellen felt her legs stilt with fear and her heart mallet against her chest. Her right hand gripped the banister to an extent that it began to ache.

And yet, she still couldn't bring herself to let go.

After a moment's hesitation, Suellen went down the stairs and continued through the kitchen doorframe to the back door. The closer she came to it, the more her body became weak with dread and made her more aware of the likely possibility that someone had followed them back from the cemetery.

Ignoring her fear, she pulled back the curtains on the door and peered outside through the glass.

"Don't open it," Andre whispered.

"I'm not going to." She gazed out at the backyard, observing every inch for movement within the shifting shadows.

"See anyone?" asked her brother, standing a distance away.

"Nope, no one," she replied. She would've almost felt better if she had seen someone out there. But seeing no one raised even more troubling questions in her mind. *Who was it? Did they follow us? Where did they go? Will they be back?*

They both took a short gasp at the sound of the refrigerator motor starting up noisily.

Suellen turned from the window and walked away. "I'm going to bed. There's no one out there."

"You sure?"

She stopped next to her brother and glanced back at the door. "Yeah. I wouldn't worry about it. If whoever that was wanted to get in, they would've done so already. Let's go before Dad wakes."

The two of them left the kitchen and hurried to the staircase. Andre went up first and continued on. He never realized his sister still stood at the bottom, staring at the back door.

She half expected to hear another knock, but only dark eerie silence invaded the house. She covered her mouth as she yawned and climbed up the stairs, eager to get some sleep.

CHAPTER 9

MONDAY AFTERNOON 3:06 P.M.

Through the windshield, Mr. Blanchard watched a crowd of middle school students cross the street. Once they reached the other side, the crossing guard lowered her handheld stop sign and walked out the street back to the curb.

Before pulling off, Mr. Blanchard waved over at the lady. She was a tall, heavy-set woman who walked with a limp. She waved back at Mr. Blanchard with a grin. "She's been crossing kids for a long time."

Riding in the backseat, Suellen combed her dark hair while gazing in a small circular mirror she held. Andre stared blankly out the front passenger window, watching the scenery go by.

Their father suddenly pressed his foot on the brakes as they approached a rough path in the street. He gently drove through it, then accelerated past it.

Suellen yawned and stretched her arms. She grabbed her backpack, stored her two items inside, and leaned her head against the door.

"What's got you down back there?" her father asked, stopping at a red light. "Your grandparents aren't that boring are they? If so, you two can come along with me and watch paint dry."

Andre laughed. "Whatever, Dad!"

Suellen saw their father's eyes on her through the rearview mirror and smiled. "I'm just tired, that's all. It's been a long Monday."

Charles grinned back then shifted his attention back on the road. Their father normally wore contacts, but today he had on glasses. Suellen's smile lasted when she noticed her father dressed in his jogging pants and white shirt. He was always so professional looking in his fire chief uniform. Whenever he wore more relaxed clothing, she found it funny.

Charles was a tall, thin, but well-built man. He had a light beard growing in that connected along his face. And his unwrinkled face made him appear younger than his 42 years of life.

"Now what's this all about?" He said, slowing the car as he stared down the road.

Suellen and Andre looked as well, and noticed the red flashing lights up ahead.

Riding along closer, they saw three police vehicles, one dark and unmarked, parked along the curb in front of the cemetery.

An officer stood center street, gesturing for them to stop.

Andre gawked back at his sister. His unblinking eyes locked onto hers.

Suellen's heart raced. *No way they can know it was us! They couldn't have seen us that night! They don't even know who we are!*

Their father eased to a stop, and the policeman strolled over to the side of the jeep.

Mr. Blanchard let down his window halfway. "Afternoon, officer."

The officer nodded his head, "Fire Chief Blanchard." He slightly leaned down to observe everyone inside. He was an older man with a heavy brown mustache. "No cause for alarm. Just checking every vehicle that passes by."

"Is there a reason for all this?" Charles asked. "I don't think I've ever seen this old place so populated."

Suellen glanced over to the funeral home, and saw the door stood wide open, revealing darkness inside.

The officer's eyes went from Andre, to Suellen, then back to their father. "Official police matter. You may proceed on now. Thank you for cooperating, Sir."

Charles briefly stared at the officer with a twisted look of bewilderment. "What's going on here? Is this something the people of the community should know about?"

The policeman's stare quickly roamed through the vehicle. As if confirming nothing was out of the ordinary, he then stood straight up and backed away. "I apologize but we're not at liberty to discuss at this moment. As I stated earlier, this is an official police matter as of now. I assure you though, the public will be notified if and when that changes. You all enjoy the rest of your day."

Charles sighed, still dissatisfied. "Alright, I understand, officer. Likewise to you." He slowly pulled off, letting his window back up as he did.

Suellen peered back and saw the officer open the driver's door to one of the vehicles and sit inside.

"Well kids, that was rather disheartening, to say the least."

"Sure was," Andre agreed. "Wish they could have told us something." He gazed back to the cemetery, but made eye contact with his sister instead. She shrugged her shoulders, just as perplexed as he was.

Their father made a left turn down a side street. "Hopefully it's nothing too serious. But whatever's going on, you kids already know the routine when you're walking home, or to school, or wherever. Be cautious of your surroundings. And walk in groups. You wouldn't believe how many crazy people are out there, just waiting for their first opportunity to abduct someone."

Andre nodded, "Alright, Dad."

Suellen folded her hands tightly together and bit her lower lip. *What was that all about? We didn't do anything that wrong to cause the police to be searching the place. Is it really that serious?*

She pressed her hands a little tighter. As much as she tried to forget what just happened, she gradually began to grow more troubled by it, almost haunted.

Leaning her head against the window, she shut her eyes, hoping to soothe her tension.

CHAPTER 10

Bright sunlight returned from behind the clouds as Mr. Blanchard pulled up in front of his parents' bi-level home. One tree stood on each side of the front yard. Most of the bare limbs were curved down, as if saddened by the change of season. Encircled around both trees was a pile of parched, dead leaves all raked up and ready to be bagged.

Suellen and Andre's grandmother, Eloise, came out of the house holding several black garbage bags. Eloise was a tall, shrewd, well aging woman in her mid-60s. She was just a few inches shorter than her son and her face had very few wrinkles. She wore a long, blue, garden apron over her jaded blue jean pants and black sweater. Her sunglasses were pulled over her short, kinky hair. She gave her guests a welcoming wave as she stepped off the front porch, taking long strides down her walkway toward the gray jeep. Andre had already opened the door and stepped out. His sister did the same, an enliven smile on her face.

"Look at you two! You're almost over my head. I might have to cut off your legs," Eloise joked.

Suellen and Andre giggled as each gave Eloise a sincere hug.

"So how was your day, Grams?" Suellen asked.

"Busy as ever. Your granddad and I have been running errands all day. Never even had a chance to turn on the television to see what's going on in the world today. I was just about to bag up these leaves out here and throw them out back. Then I was going to get to picking my green tomatoes out back and fry them up."

"I can clean up these leaves for you," Andre offered. "No trouble."

"And I'll help you pick out back," said Suellen.

"Well I sure would appreciate it. Thank you."

Eloise took notice of her grandchildren's clothing. Suellen wore a jean jacket while Andre had on a blue windbreaker.

"You two don't have anything heavier to put on?" she questioned. "It ain't that warm out here." She gave Charles a disapproving look.

"I know, Mom. I keep forgetting to pick up their heavy jackets from the cleaners. I'll get them while I'm out running errands. Where's Dad? He still coming along well?"

"By the Grace of God," his mother declared. "It's been nine months since he's been walking on his own. He's out now on one of his weekly jogs."

Charles laughed. "My old man's more active now than he was before the accident."

"You don't know the half of it," said his mother. "It's been a difficult six years, but your father was determined not to spend the rest of his life depending on a wheelchair. Anyway, you get on out of here and take care of your business. And make sure you get their good jackets, now."

"Yeah okay, thanks, Mom."

Eloise nodded and gave her son a last wave before leading her grandchildren toward the house.

Charles shifted the gear on his gray Grand Cherokee, checked his mirror, and did a U-turn in the middle of the street.

As they walked down the front path, nearing the house, Eloise handed Andre the several garbage bags she held. "It does my heart well knowing I have such thoughtful grandchildren."

Andre grinned. "Happy to oblige."

"Just say 'you're welcome' like everybody else, Einstein," Suellen remarked, rolling her eyes.

Andre purposely bumped into her, then ran off to the side near one of the trees.

"That's okay," Suellen called after him in mock anger. "I know where you live. The same place I do."

"Love you, Su," Andre replied. All three of them broke out in laughter.

When Andre opened the large bag, he grabbed a handful of leaves and began storing them inside. His grandmother and sister continued around the side of the house. "We'll be back here in the garden if you need us," Eloise said.

"Alright, Grandma." He glanced up, and watched them walk out of sight.

***

Hauling one black garbage bag over each shoulder, Andre made his way down the path in the backyard. He looked over, watching his sister and grandmother pick vegetables near the garage. The garden only occupied a small space in the backyard, but it was glorious in the eyes of Eloise. She leaned toward the ground while sitting in a chair, humming the tune *Amazing Grace*.

"These beauties were well worth the wait," she said to no one in particular." She stood up, holding a green tomato, then gently tossed it up and let it drop back into her grasp.

Andre went past them, out near the garage. He threw the bags down with the others and closed the tall wooden gate. "That's the last of the leaves out front," he announced, running the short distance to join the others.

Eloise faced him, holding in her hand a plastic bag full of big green tomatoes. Andre leaned over and took a sniff. "You ready for this good eatin', handsome?" His grandmother asked, grinning, her fist resting on her hip.

"Yes, Ma'am, these are gon' fry up real good. You need any help out here? I'm willing to do anything that'll get these tomatoes cooked up quicker."

Suellen reached down for a large brown paper bag and hauled it over with the others. "Boy, stop rushing us."

Eloise shook her head, laughing, then brushed some dirt off Andre's shirt. "We've just about gotten everything taken care of out here. Most of them are inside on the kitchen counter. But if you want, you can soak about a bag of them in water for cleaning. And get a couple skillets ready, while we finish up out here."

"Okay, I can do that." Andre jogged away toward the house and went inside, softly closing the screen door behind him. He went to the kitchen sink and quickly washed his hands. Through the window over the sink, he stared out at his sister and grandmother as they bagged the remaining green tomatoes.

Andre dried his hands and leaned toward the cabinet below for a skillet, but stopped midway after hearing the low tone of a man's voice from the next room. He twisted his face in confusion, struggling to make out the words. Steadily, he made his way toward the doorway and rounded the corner into the front room of the house.

"Granddad?" He called. "You made it back?" Staring past the long table, Andre observed the wide screen television, sitting on top of a white dresser stand up against the wall near the open doorway.

He watched as a local news anchorman reported on a story. The volume was barely audible, but at the bottom displayed in bold capital letters was: **BREAKING NEWS SEGMENT**.

He thought it odd how he hadn't initially heard the television when he came back inside, but neglected to be wary over it.

Andre continued over to the screen and grabbed the remote laying beside it. With the press of a button, it went off to a dark screen that reflected the outline of a tall man standing in the background. His face was covered by a dark ski mask.

Andre quickly wheeled around, only to see no was there anymore. He blinked several times, as if expecting the figure to reappear. His wide-eyed stare darted around the room as his jaw quivered. His feet remained rooted despite the throb of fear that crept inside him, ordering him to run.

Letting the remote fall from his grip, Andre rushed out the front door and around back, glancing behind only once to see if he was being followed.

CHAPTER 11

MONDAY AFTERNOON, 5:24 P.M.

Dribbling his basketball down the sidewalk, Brandon walked alongside his friend, Derrick Jeffers, as they headed home. Brandon turned his head and saw at a distance the many police cars and news vans jammed in front of the cemetery three blocks down. No vehicles or pedestrians could get through now.

"What do you think that's all about by that graveyard?" Derrick asked, taking a quick glance, then focusing back on his companion.

With his blue sweatshirt hanging from his head by its hood, Brandon replied, "I don't know. All I know is once again, I beat you on the court."

Derrick smiled, rubbing the top of his dark, bushy hair and stared up at the clear, dimming sky. "I almost beat you on the court this time, dude."

Brandon stopped dribbling and carried the ball under his arm. "Almost doesn't count though. I still won."

"Yeah but it wasn't an easy win. You were looking kinda tired towards the end."

Brandon threw his head back, chuckling. "Boy, please. I dribbled circles around you. Had you on the court looking all crazy. You have those big round glasses and still couldn't see what was going on."

"Shut up," Derrick said through laughter. He snatched the basketball from under Brandon's arm, but it slipped through his grip, and went rolling into the street. Immediately, Brandon chased after it, and stopped it from going too far.

"LOOK OUT!" Derrick shouted from the curb. Zooming down the street as if on a highway, was a long, red Oldsmobile that came to a screeching stop to avoid colliding into Brandon.

His reaction was much too slow. He knew if the car hadn't braked, it would've hit him dead on.

With his heart beating swiftly, he raised a trembling hand at the driver. "Sorry about that."

The car remained stagnant, its dark tinted windows preventing anyone from seeing inside. The tires and lower part of the automobile were coated with dry mud.

"Sorry," he repeated, and walked out the street.
Holding the ball under his arm again, Brandon gave the car a final glance before stepping onto the sidewalk. The vehicle didn't move. Nor did the driver attempt to scold them on their reckless behavior.

"What's their deal?" Derrick asked. "You know them or something?"

Brandon shook his head. "I don't think so. Not driving that dirt mobile anyway. I don't know why they're still sitting there."

Derrick continued to gaze at the car again as it remained stagnant. He thought about calling out to them, but decided not to. "This is getting weird. Let's go."

They continued down the pavement, constantly eyeing the road, waiting for the car to drive past. But instead, it began cruising alongside them at a slow pace. Brandon kept his eyes forward, acting as though he didn't notice. Hoping the driver would move on.

But his friend discreetly stole another glance. "Maybe they need directions. You think?" Derrick wondered, trying to be logical to chase away his sense of alarm.

"Got a strange way of going about it if so," Brandon muttered. He surveyed the area ahead of them, knowing an abduction would less likely take place with witnesses around. But his discomfort leaped to fear after realizing they were alone on the block.

They're not going to do anything, Brandon told himself. *The cops are just blocks away.*

Despite his notion, he began walking a little faster. His eyes fixed on his house as he neared it. The Oldsmobile slowed as the engine began to sputter, allowing them to get ahead before it crept on behind them. The boys stopped in front of Brandon's house and gawked at the vehicle that stalked them.

No sooner than their heads turned, the Oldsmobile roared past, went through a stop sign, and continued down the road, its engine sputtering all the way.

Derrick took off his glasses and rubbed his face, "That was really strange."

"You catch their license?" Brandon asked, switching the basketball to his left arm.

"I tried to," Derrick replied, putting his glasses back on his dark face, "but they were going too fast."

"Riding in that old, dirty, beat-up car gives Olds-mobile a whole new meaning," Brandon cracked. They both laughed, feeling at ease.

"Hey Brandon, I been meaning to ask you. Your friend Suellen. Is she— a nice person?"

"Yeah, she is. Been friends with her and Slim since fourth grade. If they can deal with me then they have to be pretty nice. Why?"

"Just asking. Are you okay though? You were almost road-kill back there."

"Yeah I'm fine," Brandon chuckled. "Will you be alright going home?"

Derrick shrugged. "I'm just a block down, I'll survive. And if that driver comes back, I'll just threaten to wash their car. Sure they'll move on then."

Brandon shook his head, snickering. "Okay, D.J. Catch you tomorrow." He gave his friend a soft punch on the shoulder, and started down the walkway leading to his house.

From somewhere above his house, a group of birds began chirping incessantly. At once, his mind recalled to the night he had viewed a strange glow inside the funeral home in the cemetery. It hadn't been in his thoughts since telling his friends on Saturday. And he had pretty much forgotten about it, finding it trivial. But since Suellen and Slim both witnessed someone there during their last visit, and now the police were apparently searching the place, Brandon was starting to think otherwise.

And then there was that car trailing us just now, Brandon said in his thoughts as he unlocked the door. He didn't know what to make of either occurrence, or how to feel about it. All Brandon knew was that things were getting more peculiar by the day.

Before entering, he looked to check on his friend, who had now made it to the next block, casually strolling along. Then, whistling a fast tune, he stepped inside, dropping his backpack and basketball by the entrance. His mother hadn't returned from her shift at the hospital, so he knew he had plenty of time to remove his belongings before she came in and started badgering him about it.

He clicked on the nearest light, which also triggered the ceiling fan, illuminating the large room from end to end. Straight ahead, around the corner from the stairs, was a tall casement cabinet. Through the glass doors were many family pictures. Carefully placed in their frames, they stood on the shelves inside. His mother had recently purchased the cabinet, so he wasn't used to seeing anything there. But already it seemed to brighten up his mood every time he saw it.

Although his parents had an amicable divorce three years prior, it was still hard on Brandon, adjusting to a new, unfortunate situation, and not having his father around as much. Seeing the portraits of them kept him grounded in the fact that they'll always be a family no matter what their circumstances.

He hurried across the wooden floor, throwing his sweatshirt on the sofa arm along the way. He continued down the hall, and into the kitchen, suddenly remembering he was supposed to take the garbage out back this morning.

If I don't do it now, I know I'll forget again and get an earful from Mom about responsibilities.

He pulled the bag up from the garbage bin by its straps, double tied it, then carried it across the room. Once opening the back door, he stepped outside to a whole new scenery from what he had last viewed.

At nearly a quarter until six, the clear sky was drenched in shades of orange and purple. The air had turned cooler, making him wish he had kept his sweatshirt with him as he ventured to the alley. A large weeping willow stood high above everything. It blocked the setting sun, casting the lawn in shadows.

His mother recently had wood fencing built in around the backyard and Brandon hadn't gotten used to it yet, either. He unhooked the latch to the gate door and swung it open, seeing the blue tin placed against the fence on the other side.

After throwing the bag inside, he pulled the garbage tin out a little further from the gate. He saw something coming and cut his eyes over to a vehicle travelling down the alleyway. His mouth dropped open. Tension constricted his body when he recognized the car at first sight.

The red Oldsmobile no longer sputtered, but the dry mud plastered along the bottom half revealed it was the same automobile from before. Brandon exited the alley as casually as possible. He made sure to slam the door so the latch on the gate would lock itself completely.

His nerves had somewhat calmed as he paced back to the house, expecting to hear the vehicle pass on by. But when the vehicle started sputtering again, he threw a glance back over his shoulder. Through the cracks between the long wooden boards, all Brandon could see were slivers of the Oldsmobile.

Initially, he hadn't been too fond of the new feature his mother had added to the backyard. But now, Brandon couldn't be more grateful for the wooden fence. It may have been the only thing protecting him.

He gradually took a retreating step, more frightened than confused as to why the driver of the vehicle continued to haunt him. His body burned with panic when he heard the car door open. He watched as something flew over the gate and landed hard on the grass lawn. He immediately recognized the halogen flashlight he had lost at the cemetery two nights ago, the bulb now shattered. Despite the cool autumn day, warm sweat formed around his forehead and slowly slid down the side of his face.

Without a second thought, Brandon sprinted off toward the house. When he hopped on the back porch, and looked back to the alley, the Oldsmobile had just pulled off, the sputtering fading away in the distance.

He continued on inside, with plans to stay there for the rest of the evening.

With his back up against the door now, he panted vigorously until he was able to move again. When he did, he began pacing the kitchen floor while cracking his knuckles, debating over whether or not to call the authorities.

I know I probably should. But what can they do? He didn't really do anything to me. Just creeped me out real bad.

Something rattled the kitchen window by the refrigerator. With much hesitance, Brandon eased his way toward it and peered out, watching the many leaves fly across the lawn and through the air as the sky grew darker.

The Oldsmobile hadn't returned, but Brandon still stood and gawked at the spot where it was. Waiting…. expecting…. fearing for its arrival.

Am I really safe? Is my mom safe? He questioned, suddenly realizing the driver now knew where he lived.

CHAPTER 12

Wordlessly staring out the window from the backseat of the car, Andre sat leaning away from his sister, who had her arm around him. Their father glanced at them through the rearview mirror as he came to a stoplight. His expression was hardened, but eyes reflected concern. "You sure you told the police everything you remembered? He didn't attack you? Or chase after you, did he?"

Still gazing out the window, not looking at anything in particular, Andre shook his head and replied softly, "No".

"What did he look like?" asked his sister.

"I don't know," her brother raised his voice. "I already told you, he had a ski mask on. When I turned around he was gone."

"Okay, alright." Suellen replied, rubbing his shoulder. She knew he was more upset than angry. But their father was quite the opposite.

Directing his attention back on the road, Charles pulled off. One hand gripped the steering wheel while the other rubbed his temple.

Calm yourself down, Dad, Suellen thought, seeing his body language. *Nobody was hurt, we're all fine. So try to calm yourself down.* She thought of his initial reaction and realized he was much more composed than he had been earlier.

Charles had returned for his children after the police had come and gone. But once learning of the break-in during his absence, he grew outraged. Hollering through the house at the top of his voice. Threatening to go down to the police station and insisting they make catching the burglar their main priority. Persuading them with a few choice words.

Charles' father was the only one who could somewhat calm his anger by reminding him he was being unreasonable and insensible. "Trust me, I understand your rage," his father Henry had said, "but going down there with all that foolishness ain't gon' solve nothing. All that'll get done is get you behind bars, Son. Now my grandson told the police everything he could recollect. Now it's up to them to do their job."

***

Charles began to relax his hold on the steering wheel. "Glad you all are okay though," he said, scratching his chin. No one spoke another word as they rode in silence the rest of the way home.

Suellen stared at her brother, who had his forehead pressed against the window. His eyes open, but inexpressive. She looked past him, to the nearly dark sky, with her mother in her thoughts. *Can't wait until Ma gets back*. She knew that having her there would make them all feel at ease, despite what happened. She couldn't stand the unsettling feeling that raided her body. Then she thought of her brother, and imagined just how frightened he must still be.

She glanced at him, then back out the window. There were no street lights around, but she knew exactly where they were. It was a route they had taken many times before, but tonight the ride back seemed strange. Or maybe it was the uneasiness that had her on edge that made things seem irregular.

She leaned her head on the back of the seat and sighed. Her eyes stayed fixed on the window, watching the night sky as they rode along in awkward silence.

CHAPTER 13

Not much had changed from the car ride once they arrived back home. After Suellen and Andre spoke with their mother, they each resided in their room, despite it being only 7:30.

As she lay on her side in bed, still wearing the clothes she had earlier, Suellen could hear the distant voice of her dad downstairs, still on the phone with her mom.

A cool autumn breeze floated through the open window at the foot of her bed. She shifted sides and laid on her back, her hands folded beneath her head as she struggled to get comfortable and relax her body and mind.

Something's just not right. It's like ever since we went to that graveyard, things have been getting....

Watching the ceiling, Suellen found herself troubled by a recent memory that left her wondering. She moved out of bed and exited the room. Rounding the corner, she strolled the short distance to her brother's room at the end of the hall near the stairway.

Without knocking, she eased her way into the half-open doorway, and saw Andre lying in bed reading a book. He had changed into black Umbro shorts and a white shirt. With one hand behind his head, he used the other to prop the book up on his chest. His stereo, placed against the wall on a small table, was turned on at a low volume.

He veered his eyes over to his sister. "Hey."

Suellen gripped the brass knob and leaned her shoulder against the door. "You doing okay?"

Andre looked off to the side, as if determining what to say to put her mind at ease. He bit his inner cheek before answering, "I'm better I guess. Can't wait until Mom gets back though."

"Yeah I know," Suellen agreed. She listened downstairs, and still heard her father on the phone.

Now's the best time. I can't hold it off any longer. "I need to talk to you, Andre."

He brought his eyes back on her now. "About what?"

She stepped further inside, continued on toward the stereo, and turned it down completely.

"What is it?" her brother asked. He closed the book and set it on the floor.

"It's about Saturday night, when we went to that cemetery."

Andre instantly rose up and sat on the edge of the bed. "Yeah, so?"

She crossed her arms and cast her gaze downward for a moment, feeling hesitant to say what was on her mind. Even to her it sounded foolish, but she couldn't help but wonder.

"I'm just saying.... there's that story about the homeless guy who was buried there years ago."

"You mean that curse or whatever about walking over his grave? You really believe that? You can't be serious, Su. Me and Brandon didn't even walk over his grave. We just looked at it. And even if we did, still you can't be serious."

"I didn't say I believed it," she said, moving closer. "All I'm saying is, ever since we went there, things have been a bit strange. And I'm not just talking about the break-in. I saw someone in that ditch with us, just like Slim saw someone in that building. Then when we got home, we heard a knock on the back door. And every police officer in town searching that area two days later. I don't know what's going on, but I'm too creeped out."

Suellen expected an immediate argumentative response. But instead Andre just stared at her with an expressionless face. She felt as though he were looking right through her.

"So....um...." he started, gathering his thoughts. "You think all that's happened has to do with us going to that old graveyard that night?"

Suellen nodded. "It's a strong possibility."

"Yeah but.... it doesn't make any sense," Andre protested. "How?"

Not knowing what to say, Suellen just shook her head solemnly.

To their surprise, the door swung open and in walked their father, his expression stern. Suellen and Andre exchanged shocked glances, both hoping he hadn't overheard their conversation.

"Hey kids, I just got off the phone with your mother. She said Granddad's transplant has been moved to tomorrow morning. He's at the hospital now getting prepped for surgery. If all goes well she'll be back by Wednesday night."

"Well that's good news," Suellen said earnestly.

"Yeah, so let's pray everything is successful," Charles replied.

"Did you tell Mom?" Andre asked. He hadn't moved from his spot on the bed.

With a sigh, Charles sauntered over to his son and sat next to him. "Yeah I did. That's why she wants to catch the next flight back as soon as she can. I told her not to worry though. But let me talk to you kids about something." He gestured for his daughter to take the seat next to him, and she obeyed.

"Kids," he said, placing his arms around their shoulders, "your old man may have overreacted today. I didn't set a very good example, and I apologize. But I'm not apologizing for caring about you two."

He shut his eyes, took in a deep breath, and continued.

"You kids know my line of work. Whether it be a burning building, an explosion, car accident, and so on, I do everything in my power to save peoples lives. But I still witness terrible things happen to other people, and people's children on a regular basis. And it breaks my heart. You understand what I'm trying to say?"

Suellen and Andre nodded. Charles pulled them closer and kissed them on the forehead.

"Alright," their father said in a more cheerful tone as he stood, "how do some classic homemade turkey burgers with freshly cut fries sound for tonight? I may need some help though. You kids know I'm all thumbs when it comes to cooking."

Andre snickered. "Okay, Dad." He followed his father out the room and down the stairs to the kitchen. Suellen continued down the hall toward her room. "I'll be down as soon as I change clothes." Although still remembering her discussion with Andre, it didn't concern her at the moment as it had before.

After the heartfelt moment with their father just now, it made things seem not as bad. A slight smile even crossed her face as she ambled on and proceeded through her open doorway.

CHAPTER 14

MONDAY NIGHT, 11:50 P.M.

Cruising down a remote road populated by trees, the red Oldsmobile traveled at a slow speed. And although nightfall had long settled, and dense fog now drifted through the air, the headlights were intentionally kept off.

Doing more thinking than focusing on the obscured road, the driver slammed on the brakes, and shut the vehicle off. He slapped the steering wheel three times with an open hand.

I should've ran him down when I had the chance! He was right in the middle of the street! It would've been so simple! Just like all the other times! So simple! They got what they deserved, every last one of them. And so will these no good whelps.

It's their own fault, but they'll get what's coming to them in good time. And if anyone gets in my way, I'll deal with them as well.

His warped mind changed his whole demeanor, as it often had in the past. *And once I'm finished, I'm out of here for good.*

A cruel smile reflected in the rear-view mirror as the driver pulled a cigarette out the console. He covered it with his hand, lit it up, and stepped out of the vehicle.

Walking around to the back of the Oldsmobile, he blew smoke from his mouth and started into the dark woods. It was a route he had taken many times since arriving in town. He knew his way around without being on a path.

Hiking through the woods, the man continued smoking. The cigarette hanging from his lips, while he rested his hands in the center pocket of his hooded sweatshirt. He rethought every step of his tactic, an impending plot inhabiting his mind.

It's a shame they're so young and not even going to get a chance to live. But they brought this on themselves that night they decided to intrude. If they think they're scared now, I'll show them what true fear is. They haven't even begun to see the worst of me.

He chuckled menacingly, then flicked the cigarette butt off into the night.

CHAPTER 15

TUESDAY MORNING, 7:55 A.M.

Suellen had awakened to the sounds of birds chirping in the tree outside her bedroom window. After getting herself ready for school, she took a moment and stood staring at her outfit in her closet door mirror. The pink rain slicker she wore added flair to her blue school uniform.

The chirping outside resurfaced and Suellen stepped over to the window, watching the same pair of birds continue their conversation on a branch. The fog from the previous night had now lifted, but overhead, heavy clouds threatened rain.

But despite the gloomy conditions, her mind was more at ease than it had been yesterday. She wasn't sure if it was the talk her father had with them, the surprisingly good night sleep she had, or the fact that it was a brand new day, but her mood had made a complete 360 in a matter of hours.

Really no sense in worrying and speculating when I don't even know what's going on. Everyone's okay, no one got hurt, that's what's important. She turned her attention back to the tree and noticed the two birds had flown off.

A knock from behind made her spin around to the open doorway where her father stood. She was surprised to see him in his navy blue khakis and white buttoned up shirt.

"You going in to work today?" she asked, staring at the gold fire chief badge on the left side of his shirt.

"I am," he replied. "I wish arsonists were more considerate of my time off. But what can you do?"

Her eyes widened. "What happened?"

"Someone reported a fire over on the other side of town in the Forest Preserve. Some locals were able to put it out before my people got there. Still need to go check it out though, and do some minor work. I'll be headed to the scene right after I drop you two off."

Suellen could hear the wind whistling through her room from the window. Rubbing her left arm, she moved closer and asked, "How'd it get started?"

"No definitive word on that yet, from what I can gather so far, it was most likely an accident. But whoever set it had no business being there in the middle of the night to begin with. We'll be out as soon as your brother finishes getting dressed."

The phone rang and Charles rushed to his room next door to answer it. "Suellen, go downstairs and bring in the newspaper before it gets soaked," he instructed before answering the call.

"Will do." She grabbed her backpack off the bed, threw it over her right shoulder, and exited her bedroom.

In the room adjacent to hers, Charles was speaking on the phone with a colleague as his daughter passed by.

As she reached the curving stairway and started down, her stomach began to rumble. *I don't think I've ever been this hungry in my life!*

All was quiet and darkened at the bottom of the stairs. The drapes were closed and no lights had been turned on. The overcast sky made the house appear depressing, almost lifeless.

Dad must really be in a rush, she thought, edging toward the front door. *Didn't even have time to watch the morning news.*

A shrill and bitter fall wind greeted Suellen as she pulled open the door. The breeze whipped across the lawn and blew wildly at her hair. When she leaned down and grabbed the newspaper off the porch, her eyes inadvertently ran across the front page headline. And her eased mind shifted to building tension.

Not a sound left her closed lips, and hardly a breath escaped from her quivering jaw as Suellen noticed the black and white mug shot of a man just above the article. She then silently read the caption one last time.

LOCAL COPS HUNT FOR KILLER AT LARGE.

CHAPTER 16

The strong gusts began to carry rain. Suellen cringed before returning inside with the newspaper in hand. The room seemed to have grown darker than before. She flicked on the nearest light switch and resumed her reading. Below the headline, in smaller type, was a sub-headline that read:

Psychopath Fugitive believed to be residing in Midwest.

With a pounding heart, Suellen began to read the narrative in silence.

Albert M. Sanderson, serving a 70-year sentence for murdering seven women in Texas over an eight month period last year, made a daring escape this past August while being transported to another penitentiary.

Police now have reason to believe he is in hiding in Millersville, Indiana after searching the funeral home of Georgia Parish Cemetery. This past weekend, officer's spotted suspicious activity on the premises. There they discovered old photos Sanderson had saved of his victims.

According to police sources, the escaped prisoner had made the abandoned cemetery his temporary hideaway, having with him a sleeping bag, pillow, blanket, and candles that had been lit, all of which are now in custody along with the photos.

Sanderson, 51, is considered a deranged serial killer who often refers to himself as 'Night Ghost,' leaving the message, 'Night Ghost Strikes' written in his victims' blood at every crime scene. Sanderson is known for stalking his victims and photographing them from a distance prior to his attack.

"We're asking that all residents in Northwest Indiana as well as the Chicagoland area be vigilant of their neighborhood," Police Chief Joshua Dawson told the press. "We do not believe he has harmed anyone since his getaway. But we are asking the public to report any suspicious behavior. This man may be armed and is extremely dangerous. If anyone even thinks they see this man, please do not approach him. Just contact the local authorities immediately." When asked if the town would have to be shut down, Dawson stated it was in consideration.

Authorities are working around the clock to keep residents safe and apprehend Sanderson, who fled from a prison bus in Redson, Texas after it crashed off the road, killing three prisoners.

The driver, Frederick Lee Blackwell, 48, stated that he was abruptly cut off by a gray Oldsmobile, and lost control trying to avoid colliding with the other vehicle. This caused the bus to flip over and slide into a ravine.

After quickly escaping out the emergency exit, Sanderson was seen getting into the passenger side of the automobile, and fleeing the scene. Police believe he is still using the same vehicle. His accomplice and long-time girlfriend, Martha Hayes, 45, was arrested after being spotted in a Memphis, Tennessee mall in September. She is currently in jail and facing charges.

As for the whereabouts of Sanderson, local police believe he has fled from the town of Millersville, but may still be in the surrounding area.

After reading the article only once, Suellen was rendered speechless. Her mind flooded with many thoughts as things started to make sense.

Feeling overwhelmed, she felt her eyes grow heavy from staring at the newspaper, until the black printed words all blurred together in her vision.

Not knowing what else to do, she just stood still, silent, and in deep thought, mulling over everything that had taken place.

It was him. He's the one who me and Slim saw inside the funeral home. And in the ditch with us. He knocked on our back door that night. He must have followed us back and…. Oh God he knows where we live! He knows where my grandparents live! It was him who broke in their house yesterday!

The more that came to mind, the more she shook her head. Her lips were trembling and she suddenly felt watched. She looked up and saw her brother gazing at her with narrowed eyes from the bottom of the stairs. He had never seen his sister in such a state of fear.

"Suellen, what's wrong?" he asked, zipping up his leather jacket halfway.

She didn't know where to start. Her mind was so overwhelmed and her body felt weak. After a short moment, she replied softly, "We're in deep trouble, Andre."

She held the newspaper out for him. He was hesitant, but he soon descended the stairs and neared his sister. Then, little by little, he slid the newspaper from Suellen's grip, and began to read.

CHAPTER 17

Hours later, Suellen ran down the school hall after the eighth grade lunch bell had rung. With her literature book in hand, and backpack on her shoulders, she sped past a long row of lockers. As she ran, she dodged collisions with several students as most were headed in the opposite direction.

After arriving at school that morning, she'd seen Slim and Brandon only minutes before class started. Since they both shared first period, Suellen gave them the front page paper to read, then arranged to meet in the library during lunch.

The crowd in the hallway was starting to thin as the students made their way to the cafeteria. Normally, Suellen would be among them, chatting about different things that happened during the day up to this point, and joking around. But today was different. Today she had too much on her mind to even pay attention to the conversations around her. Her tension-filled mind tuned everyone out.

She made a sharp right turn and came up along the glass wall that separated the library from the hallway. Slim, who was coming down the other end of the hall, met up with her at the double doors.

"This is bad," Slim said with a worried expression. She tugged at the sleeves of her baby blue sweatshirt tied at her waist over her light brown khakis and blue sweater before entering the library. Suellen followed close behind her.

The large room was quiet and empty. The only other person around was the librarian, who was standing behind her desk way on the far right side. Staring at her computer screen and typing away, she didn't seem to notice them at all.

Suellen and Slim sauntered off to the left where two rows of long tables were placed. The girls sat side by side at the nearest one.

"I read the paper first, then gave it to Brandon," Slim told her. "He'll bring it when he comes."

Suellen placed the literature book she carried on the table and sighed. "I'm not even sure I want it back."

"My parents had just heard about it when your dad called us this morning. They want me to stay at your place until they get off today." She paused, and stared off for a moment. It was difficult for her to bear the danger they were all in. Just the thought of it weighed her down in a heap of dread.

"When I found out, I really wanted to tell my parents. About everything. I almost did, but....how did we get ourselves in this mess Su?"

Suellen responded with a shrug, not knowing at all what to say. "My dad spoke to Ms. Dowell too. She wants Brandon to come over until she gets home."

"Here he comes now," said Slim, staring past her friend into the hall.

Looking over her shoulder, Suellen saw Brandon jog past them. He pushed open one of the doors and came inside. Spotting the girls right away, he hurried over and sat across from them. The paper, Suellen saw, was rolled up in his hand.

He slammed it down on the table and said rather loudly, "You can't be serious. This is beyond crazy."

"There's more," Suellen replied in a lower tone. "He's been stalking us. Ever since we went there Saturday night. He knocked on our door that night. And yesterday, he broke into my grandparents' house when we were there."

"Say what now," Slim remarked, facing her.

Suellen nodded. "Andre saw him and we called the police. By the time they came and searched the place, he was gone."

Neither Slim nor Brandon gave a verbal response. They just sat with their eyes locked on her, while she stared down at the rolled up paper.

Brandon leaned back in his chair and let out a low groan. He covered his face up with his hands and slowly slid them away, letting them fall on the table.

On the other side, the librarian had ceased her typing, leaving the room in a peace-less quiet that was almost intolerable.

"Well, looks like this Sanderson lunatic had a busy day yesterday," said Brandon. "I think he almost ran me over. Me and D.J. were walking home, and I ran out in the street to get my basketball. I didn't see it coming, but this Oldsmobile nearly hit me." He leaned forward with folded hands, then shifted his eyes from Suellen to Slim. Their faces stayed on his, unmoving.

"Then he rode beside us down the sidewalk. Thinking about it now, I probably shouldn't have went home. But I did and he drove off. Next thing I know…. when I go and take the garbage out…. I see the same car coming down the alley. It just sat there at first. Then the flashlight I lost that night came flying over the gate, broken."

Slim gasped, and threw a hand over her mouth.

"And when he finally drove off, I didn't know what to think. Or do. I tried not to make too much of it. But now…." He slightly scrunched up his brow, reflecting upon everything. "We're in it deep huh?"

No one answered. Slim stared off to the side, shaking her head. "I don't understand why he doesn't just leave town. If the cops know he's here and how he's getting around, he can't be that hard to spot. And he has to know that."

"Yeah but we were at the cemetery that night," Suellen replied. "The police came there because they saw us trespassing. We lured them to his hideaway. That's why he's after us."

"Or he could've been just trying to scare us," Slim argued. "For all we know, Sanderson could be long gone by now."

Suellen shook her head slowly. "He's not. People like him aren't right in the head." She stared up at the ceiling. Contemplating whether or not to tell them what her father had informed her of this morning.

"When I showed the paper to my dad, it took everything in him not to flip out. He called everyone he could and told them about it. His parents, your parents, my mom, everyone. That's why I didn't have a chance to see you before first hour.

"Then he had to go into work today. Someone had set a fire in the forest preserve last night. Nobody got hurt, but there were fresh tire tracks found back up in there on the dirt road. Cops found out that they belong to an Oldsmobile."

With her arms folded on the table, Slim turned and looked away. "I don't know," she muttered in a tone that was barely audible. "I just don't know. Is your dad still picking us all up after school, Su?"

"If he can get away from working on his week off, then yeah. And my grandparents both have doctor's appointments today. But he said not to wait too long for him, and to just walk together if he's not here right away."

"Wait a sec. Wait a sec," Brandon said. He snatched up the paper, unfurled it, and began to skim through it. "Where is it? Where is it?" He whispered, running his eyes up and down the page. Placing the newspaper on the table, he spun it around to where they could read it, and with the tip of a finger, pointed out a paragraph.

"Right here, it says it was a gray Oldsmobile that cut the guy off on the road. But the one me and D.J. saw yesterday was red."

The girls leaned forward, and quickly read the selected paragraph.

"He painted it," Slim said looking back up.

Brandon leaned back in his seat and nodded. "The police don't even know what he's driving."

Suellen's temper flared. She crumpled the paper up in her fist and squeezed it, then tossed it to the other side of the table. But that did nothing to ease the fear that plagued her mind.

CHAPTER 18

A small group of students entered the library chatting and giggling. Suellen and her friends were completely oblivious of their entrance. Without looking their way, the four girls went off to the opposite side of the room and sat by the computers to begin working on a project.

Brandon glanced at his wristwatch. "It's twelve-fifteen. Got a half hour of lunch left if you two want to head to the cafeteria. You know.... try and forget all this. At least for a little while."

With distraught eyes directed at the balled up paper on the table, and a fist pressed against her jaw, Suellen gazed through the glass and out into the empty hallway. The hunger she usually felt around this time of day was now replaced with a knot of fear in her abdomen. "You all can go if you want. I don't really have an appetite now."

"I don't think I can ever forget something like this," Slim said. She moved her long hair over to her right shoulder and with both hands, began twisting it gently. "We can't pretend like nothing's happening, Brandon. We need to go to the police with this."

"Yeah but," he stopped mid-sentence, watching the librarian who had suddenly appeared. She bent down to the lower shelves that ran along the glass wall and began stacking books. Brandon leaned in closer on the table and said in a soft voice, "If we go to the police, we'll have to explain that we were the ones they saw that night. Cause they'll want to know how we know all this."

Still playing with her hair, Slim shrugged. "If we have to then we'll just tell them. This is too important not to."

Brandon looked and saw the librarian had moved from her previous spot. Nevertheless, his voice remained low. "Right. And then they lock us up for trespassing. And just like that, we all have criminal records."

Slim narrowed her eyes, giving him a scornful glare. "Are you forgetting we're in this mess because of you? You were the one who just had to go there. The whole town is in danger, not just us. You'd think after knowing all that, you wouldn't be so selfish." Reaching down, Slim snatched up her backpack and stormed off.

Brandon watched as she passed him, his eyes filled with hurt.

Listening to everything, Suellen moved her hand from her cheek and sighed miserably.

"I'm guessing you're mad at me too, huh," Brandon assumed, avoiding eye contact. "I never meant to…. I mean I didn't know that…. it's just that…."

"She's not mad at you," Suellen assured him. "She's just… mad at the situation. Like we all are."

"Yeah but she's right though. It *is* my fault. If I hadn't been dead-set on seeing that tombstone then…."

"It doesn't matter, Brandon. That's over and done with. We've got much bigger problems now. And we can't keep this to ourselves any longer. I should've told my dad everything this morning. Whatever consequences we face, at least we'll be alive to face them."

He looked at her, and nodded.

It's going to be alright. Suellen told herself. *Once we tell our parents, they can notify the police and they can take it from there. Sanderson won't be any trouble to find when they know he had is car painted. Everything will be alright now.*

She rubbed a hand against the side of her head, struggling to keep from crying.

CHAPTER 19

Now at the end of the day, Suellen stood by her open locker and placed one last book into her backpack. She slid both arms through her pink rain slicker, then slammed the door shut without observing herself in the mirror. She was in no mood for that at all.

With her backpack in hand, she leaned her back against the wall of lockers and longed for everything around to be drowned out. The talking, the crowded halls, the apprehension to be no more. If only for a brief moment.

But the turmoil within her wouldn't allow it. Instead, the chaos seemed to build and twist internally, bringing her much distress. Her head was aching terribly. And being in a hall full of everyone chatting and gossiping away wasn't making it any better.

Through the several students strolling down the hallway, she spotted Andre hurrying over towards her. "I spoke with Brandon before seventh period," she heard him say. "He told me about last night. And what you all talked about during lunch today."

Suellen tossed her backpack across one shoulder. "As soon as I see Dad, I'm telling him, Andre. Whether you're with me on this or not."

He rubbed the top of his smooth head. "Well, to be honest, I think we should've said something yesterday. He's probably been following us for days now. We can't keep quiet about this. I don't know what we were thinking. But I do know that Dad's going to be heated at us for not telling him right away."

Suellen nodded. "Yeah he is. But in this case, we just got to pick our poison."

Tilting his head back, Andre let out a long, exasperated sigh.

The several conversations in the hall gradually fizzled out when the principal's voice emerged on the intercom. "Attention students, I would like to remind all of you who are walking home to do so in pairs of two or more. Do not, I repeat do not walk home alone or talk to anyone of whom you don't know. Thank you. And please be safe, everyone."

By the time the announcement ended, the packed hallway was beginning to clear out and Suellen stepped onward to the center. She stared down either end of the hall. Most of her dark brown hair rested on her right shoulder as she spun her head one final time. There was no sign of her father.

Slim and Brandon surfaced from around the nearest corner and continued closer. He threw his arm around her shoulder and flashed a thumbs up. "Everything's cool this way. Right, Slim?"

She playfully shoved him away in response, making him drop his brown leather coat he'd held. Without stopping, he scooped it up and tossed it over his left shoulder.

Suellen displayed a grin. It was the first time she had all day. Andre stepped up beside his sister as Slim and Brandon made their way over.

"Looks like we're stuck walking today," Andre said. "No different from any other day, I guess."

"Except now we have a serial killer hunting us down." Brandon replied. "Doesn't get any worse than that."

Suellen stared at him and thought, *It's so different seeing Brandon like this. He's usually always laughing, cracking jokes, or just being goofy. Now he's almost humorless and downhearted. He's nothing like himself. I want my old friend back.*

"Let's get going, guys," Slim said as she buttoned the collar of her baby blue trench coat. "I'm ready to get this over with."

Suellen eyed the clock-face overhead and saw it was almost a quarter after three. Great discomfort suddenly took a toll on her. She wanted to continue waiting, in hopes that her dad would show soon, but her better judgment spoke against it. And with darkness approaching within the next hour, she wanted to get on home.

She shut her eyes, and said a quick prayer to herself before leading them off down the hall toward the exit.

***

They had gone almost two blocks when the cold air began to reach through their coat layers. The air was gentle. But the temperature had dropped dramatically since early that morning. And now, gray ominous snow clouds covered the sky.

A distance ahead of them, groups of other students were walking in the same direction, but that did nothing to ease the silent tension among them.

"There should be more law enforcement around," said Slim, her words muffled by the scarf shielding her mouth. "I've only seen one police car go by so far."

"That's probably because according to the paper, he's already fled from here," Brandon replied as they stopped at the curb.

On the next block, right on the other side of the street, was the cemetery, it's overgrown grass swaying in the light draft. It was their first time seeing the cemetery since all the media coverage it had gotten within the last few days. Now there were no police vehicles, no news reporters, and no one else around but them.

Hanging in the middle of the door, from end to end, was a large sign that read CONDEMNED. The two trees on each side stood on guard, giving the building an even more daunting appearance.

"I can't take this anymore!" Brandon announced through gritted teeth. He broke away from the group and darted across the street toward the graveyard. With one leap, he hopped the fence and started down the center path to enter the decrepit building.

CHAPTER 20

Suellen, Slim, and Andre chased after Brandon, until they reached the fence.

"What is he.... is he trying to.... why did....?" Suellen exclaimed, out of breath. All she could do was watch with a wrinkled forehead as her friend neared the old building.

"Boy, are you crazy?!" Slim raised her voice over the fence.

Brandon said not a word as he pushed against the door with his shoulder. After his fifth try, the entrance slowly began to give in.

"Brandon, no!" Suellen exclaimed. Instinctively, she slid open the gate and rushed over. Slim and Andre reluctantly followed.

Suellen caught up to Brandon first and grabbed his wrist. He turned to face her. "What?"

"After everything that went on, you're trying to go up in there!" She scolded him.

Brandon sighed, and gently pulled his arm away. "You don't understand, Su. I heard someone screaming in there."

"You did?" Suellen faced the door and listened. Her eyes broadened and she stepped back. "I hear it too."

"If someone's in there the only thing we can do is tell the police." Slim remarked. "We can't go exploring in there and put our own lives at risk. Even if Sanderson's not in there, the fact that he was should be enough to not even want to be near this old place."

"I'm not afraid of him," Brandon retorted. "In fact I'm hoping he is in there. This guy wants us to be afraid of him. That's how losers like him are. I won't give him that power, though."

"So what are you going to do, challenge a grown man? What are you trying to prove?" questioned Slim.

"That he can't just stalk us.... follow us home.... and break into our house and get away with it. This guy knows who we are. Where we live. And he's gonna be coming for us real soon. And now he's probably got someone locked away in here. We can't just leave them. What if it were one of us? I wouldn't want someone to ignore my screams. And I'm sure you feel the same way!"

"But look what they put on the door," said Andre. "They wouldn't condemn this place for nothing. The door's probably bolted shut now because it's too dangerous. It's not worth it."

Brandon ignored him and grunted as he continued to shove the door open wide enough to enter. He shifted his attention to his three companions and sighed at their disapproval expressions. "I'm not asking for you all to agree, or even to come with me. Just...."

He froze after observing a red automobile barrelling down the road two blocks away. "That's him coming now!"

Suellen and the others stared in the direction of his gaze, and panicked. They knew if he spotted them, there'd be no telling what he might do.

Having no other options, they were forced to follow Brandon into the old structure.

Once inside, Brandon, Andre, and Slim slammed the door shut and backed away, invading the building with cold darkness. Through vague vision, Suellen staggered her way over to the window. The carpeted floor beneath them was damp, and sent a foul odor through the air. As her eyes adjusted, she was able to spot debris that had fallen over the years.

After many careful steps, she reached the window, which was nothing more than a large square opening in the building now, and peeked around the corner to the street outside. She pressed her mouth shut to avoid making any sound that could draw unwanted attention their way. The sound of the vehicle getting closer flooded her ears. Her heartbeat hammered through her chest so intensely it was almost painful. The backpack on her shoulders felt like it weighed a ton. She flinched when the car rolled into view.

"It's not him," she informed them before turning away.

Pressed back against the wall, she allowed her eyes to wander the room while she unflustered her thoughts. The space was large and empty. To the far right was a fragment of a built-in receptionist desk. The other half lay adjacent to it in a hefty pile of old wood. "That was an old red station wagon. Not an Oldsmobile."

Slim and Andre both sighed in much relief.

"Hello? Is anyone here?" Brandon called out. "It's okay. We can help you."

They all listened for a fair amount of time but the silence remained. No birds....or crickets.... only quiet.

"No one's here but us," Slim remarked.

Brandon rubbed the back of his neck. "But I'm almost sure I heard a scream. You said you heard it.... right, Su?"

"I know I did," she whispered.

Andre crumpled up his face. "Let's just get out already. This smell is about to kill me."

Slim was first to pace toward the exit. "What's this?" She stopped to peel off some debris she had stepped in. But in her hand, she held a short stack of papers.

"What are those?" Andre asked, stepping beside her.

Slim eyed one close to her face and saw nothing but white. "I have no idea. But they feel new. Doubt they've been here all this time."

Suellen and Brandon strolled over and crowded behind the others. Fading sunlight poked through the clouds and poured into the room through the broken windows. Slim flipped one of the papers over and right away recognized the image on the other side. "It's a picture of us!"

"Of us?" Suellen leaned over her friend's shoulder to examine it more closely. Her mouth dropped open.

Andre observed the pictures as well. "This is from when we were hiding behind the tree that night. Sanderson must've been.... watching us.... from here."

"There's more," Slim said.

They all watched in stunned silence as one by one, she went through three more photos with them in it.

"But....how?" Suellen questioned, her voice shaking.

"There's something else on the floor." Andre said, looking down. "I can hear it."

He reached down and came up with a small object in hand. He held it up to his face and could still barely see it. But he could feel that it was covered with many scratches. "It's an old voice recorder."

He played with one of the lower buttons and the device cut on.

"*September twentieth, two thousand six,*" said a deep, rough voice on the recorder. The next sound that came through was a hysterical woman, crying and whimpering. The woman's voice jumped and skipped a few times before her wretched scream came blaring through the recorder. Andre dropped it and the device shut off.

No one said anything for several seconds. The empty room was now silent, and yet it wasn't. For the audio of the woman's scream of terror still lived on past its cessation.

"What in the world...?" Slim started.

"That's the scream I heard," Brandon quickly answered. "It must have.... gone off.... I guess...." His voice trailed off as he began to fathom what they had just heard on the recorder: a woman being murdered.

The room fell quiet again, as if the woman's scream had somehow paralyzed them. It was so loud, so frightening, so demoralizing, the sound of it would forever be engraved in their memory.

"That recording is from over three years ago," Suellen stated, feeling a rush of nausea. "But the paper said he killed seven women last year alone."

"Maybe the police don't know about this one," said Slim. "What if he's killed more women than they realize?"

"But they searched the place," Andre said, staring down at the voice recorder. "How could they miss this?"

With narrowed eyes, and a soaring temper, Brandon still gawked at the snapshots. "They didn't. He must have come back after they left."

Suellen gasped and covered her mouth as she continued to stare at the photos. *He was actually here. We're standing in a place a serial killer once used as his hideout. What if he comes back? Or never left?* Her legs started to grow weak and she knew in her heart she didn't want to be there.

"I thought you said it couldn't get any worse," Andre remarked to Brandon.

"Until it does," Brandon replied, and sauntered off. "Put those pictures back on the floor. He can't know that we were in here."

A low creaking began above them. Slim dropped the photos as if they were burning, looking up with a short gasp. The small amount of light inside revealed a ceiling layered with cobwebs. She shuddered at the sight, then turned away.

At the exit, Brandon grabbed the knob and pulled at the door, only to discover it wouldn't budge. He tugged four more times, harder with each yank, with no success. Clouds hovered over the sun. The room dimmed as shifting shadows lengthened throughout the space.

Overhead, a loud groaning erupted through the ceiling. Brandon backed off the door and neared the others. And as he did, a large, heavy piece of the ceiling collapsed and slammed onto the floor. Dirt, wood, and other debris seemed to shower down from all sides as though a bomb had gone off, sending clouds of dust throughout the gloomy room.

"BACK UP!" Brandon shouted over the thunderous rumbling.

They all scampered further into the empty room as the roof caved in.

CHAPTER 21

With eyes shut tight and head turned to the side, Suellen shielded her face with an arm. Her heartbeat was rapid with terror. And although the noises overhead had ceased, her knees buckled until she could barely stand. Her bones felt soft and brittle. She partly wondered if she had been crushed.

"Everybody alright?" Brandon asked from beside her.

"I guess," Slim coughed, then began brushing debris off her coat.

A cold breeze pierced the air. Suellen uncovered her face and gasped after seeing the giant gap in the roof. The floor ahead of them was littered high with fallen wreckage from the ceiling and roof.

Andre wiped his forehead with the back of his hand. "There's no way to get over there to the door. Not even the window!"

Slim gazed around the room, her thoughts growing so frantic she began to talk fast. "Well we got to do something! No one knows we're here! And we can't just wait around for the whole building to collapse on us!"

Panting heavily, Brandon stepped back and observed the large gap in the roof. "There's got to be a way out of here." He kept a calm expression to conceal the panic that riveted him.

"There's a door back here," Andre pointed out.

Hidden within shadows in the back of the room was a closed door. It leaned forward and only hung from the bottom hinge. Without a second thought, everyone launched in that direction.

Pushing against the dust-smeared door, Suellen eased the entrance open little by little. The bottom scrapped against the floor before it came to a standstill halfway open.

The doorway led into a small bare room which was once an office. The only thing it contained was an open fireplace on the far left side. But what got their attention was the smashed window further down near the corner. A jagged row of broken glass lined the bottom of the windowsill.

"Let's go," Suellen exclaimed, scurrying towards the window with the others behind her. The soles of their shoes crunched down on chunks of busted glass. Suellen climbed up on the ledge first and quickly jumped through the window. She landed to the side near the tree that stood in back.

Slim leaped out afterwards, her hat falling off when she hit the ground. She snatched it up and put it back on. Andre was next. He wiped his sweaty palms dry on his pant legs and hurried onto the ledge. As he squatted in the opening, a crash broke out behind him. The building began to shake as the remainder of the roof disintegrated.

Slim's eyes began to tear up. "NO NO NO!"

"JUMP!" Suellen screamed.

With trembling legs, Andre jumped outside. Brandon dove out right after him, the cool air was refreshing against his warm body. As he climbed to his feet, he stared back at the old funeral home that had nearly buried them all alive. Through the window, he saw that the roof was no more. Piles and piles of scattered fragments lay littered high about the building.

Out of breath, he stared at Suellen, Slim, and Andre, who had their eyes on him as well.

"You okay?" Suellen asked.

Brandon nodded. Feeling guilty, he lowered his head and moved past them. He started down the steep hill with the others following behind. The day had nearly grown dark and now sleet was starting to fall from the thick layer of gray clouds. Moving fast down the grassy slope, more frozen rain began to strike their faces as the sleet came down harder. Suellen winced when a sharp winter breeze blew against them making the old unstable building grumble above them.

Reaching the bottom, they ran across the ditch. Bare tree limbs brushed against them as they crossed to the other side. The crackle of dead leaves beneath their feet was the only sound that invaded the area.

Andre tripped over a rock and almost went sailing to the ground. But Brandon caught him by the arm and prevented his fall in time.

They struggled up the hill, tired, but also determined to get as far away as possible from the old building. Soon after making it onto the sidewalk, they stopped to take a short breather.

Suellen set her hands on her hips, trying to keep from collapsing. With her aching legs and chest feeling like it was only seconds from exploding, her body had never been in so much pain.

"I feel — like — I'm about — to vomit," Andre said in between breaths.

"You and me both," Brandon replied.

Slim took her hat off and fanned herself with it despite the cold. "We better get going before it gets dark."

Suellen faced the other side of the street and stared at the houses. Most were either one story or bi-level, but still looked to be in excellent condition.

I don't care how nice they are on the inside. Why would anyone want to live in a house where you can look out the window and see this place every day? It took her a moment to calm herself, grateful they had all made it out.

They rested for only a moment longer before moving on. With their sneakers slapping against the slick pavement, the four of them continued to run down the block.

They had nearly reached the street when Suellen felt the ground slide beneath her. She skidded for less than five seconds before losing her balance and landing hard on her face in the street. Her body screamed with discomfort.

But soon, her shriek echoed throughout the neighborhood when she saw the car rolling straight towards her.

CHAPTER 22

Seized with terror, Suellen froze as the driver struggled to stop. The tires squealed on the slick road, but the vehicle kept edging closer. A bulge of dismay attacked her heart, paralyzing her as she watched the car barrel sideways into the middle of the street. Finally, the driver was able to brake completely, but Suellen still lay there, unable to move. Andre, Slim, and Brandon ran into the street and helped pull her off the ground.

"You okay?" Andre asked, wrapping her in a hug.

Suellen wiped the cold tears from her face and forced a grin. "Yeah, I'm fine."

The driver of the vehicle hopped out. She was a tall woman, with kinky auburn hair that bounced as she rushed over.

"Oh my Lord, child! Are you alright?" the woman asked sincerely. She kneeled down in her long white trench coat and rested a hand on Suellen's shoulder. "Well that was a foolish question, of course you're not. I know I wouldn't be. And look, you're shaking. Are you hurt? Let me take you to the hospital."

Suellen gently pulled away from the woman. "You don't have to. I'll be fine."

"Are you sure?" her brother asked. "That was a pretty hard fall you took."

"I'm not hurt. Just a little shook up." She looked down and pulled a damp leaf off her pink rain slicker.

The woman shifted her eyes past Suellen and waved her arm. "Everybody's okay here, thanks!"

They all turned and realized she was speaking with some residents who had heard screaming and came outside. The spectators watched a bit longer then slowly returned to their homes.

"So glad you're not hurt, child. I thank the Lord I saw you in time and wasn't distracted." The woman then stood back up. "Well, if you don't need to go to the hospital, at least let me take you all home."

"Uh…. sure," Suellen replied, not wanting to be rude. She strolled to the gray Malibu and got in the front seat. Andre, Slim, and Brandon climbed in the backseat while the woman got back behind the wheel. Her windshield wipers were on a slow rotation.

"It's not too hot in here for you is it? I always like to stay toasted this time of year."

"No, we're good," Andre replied.

"This is very nice of you," Slim said, as the car pulled off.

The woman continued down Rainey Avenue until gently braking at a stop sign.

"Oh it's no trouble at all. What street do you all stay on?"

"We all stay three blocks down on the next street over. On Mort Road," said Suellen, pointing.

The lady nodded and made a left turn. "I was just listening on the radio about that God-awful serial killer that was hiding out here. Supposedly he's fled the town. Now I try to see the good in people. But this man… he doesn't even seem human. Murdering over half a dozen women because he blamed them for being more successful than he was. That's just a downright shame. Then the fool wants to be called 'ghost in the night' or some nonsense like that."

The lady shook her head in disgust. "I'm sure my grandfather was turning over in his grave the whole time that criminal was there hiding out."

Suellen spun her head over. "Your grandfather?"

Watching the road, the lady smiled. "Robert Otis Caldwell. I'm sure you've heard ridiculous stories about his grave being cursed. Don't believe any of it. He was a kind man. But after my father was born, he lost his job and made the mistake of walking out on his family."

"Why'd he do that?" Andre asked, leaning forward between the two front seats.

"He felt ashamed and downhearted. Like he wasn't capable of taking care of his own family. So I guess he felt the best option was to leave. And that's what got him killed on the streets."

No one said anything. Frankly, no one knew exactly how to respond. Suellen just stared at the vent, listening to the heat blow out. She felt compelled to say something— she just didn't know what.

"His headstone was a John Doe for quite a while," the lady continued. "My dad always worked odd jobs and was never able to replace it. But once I started my career and started saving, I gave him a proper one.

"Then here comes this no good fool, hiding up in the place! Just no respect at all! That kind of incivility really gets under my skin. When they catch him, he needs to be thrown under the prison. But I pray the Lord delivers him from that murderous spirit."

She was nice enough to give us a ride. Suellen thought, feeling terrible. *We can't just sit here being quiet while she's talking to us.*

"I know. That's crazy," she finally said.

"What were you all running for? No one was bothering you kids were they?"

"We....we're.... just ready to get inside," Brandon told her.

The woman threw her head back, laughing as she brought the car to a stop. "I understand that. I'm not trying to be out any longer than I have to in this weather. Let's see.... Mort Road.... so I need to make a left?"

"Yes Ma'am," Suellen answered. "We can hop out at the next stop sign."

The vehicle was silent from then on. The only noise came from the high blowing heat and the low jazz music on the radio. Suellen desperately wanted for one of them to think of something to say. Just to make light conversation. *Maybe I should've got in the back.*

Feeling awkward, she roamed her eyes around the vehicle. Hanging from the rearview mirror was an employee identification card inside a small plastic case. Suellen studied the card and read the lady's name and title to herself.

Evelyn N. Belfield
Senior Mortgage Loan Officer at Millwood Midwest Mortgages.

The woman pulled to the side when she reached the next corner. "Alright now, you kids be careful out here. Get on home before it gets any darker."

"We will," Suellen stated, as they scooted out. "Thanks again."

"Yeah, we really appreciate it, Ma'am," Brandon added.

Evelyn winked at him and smiled. "No problem Sweetheart. You all be safe now."

Brandon smiled back, slammed the back door, and stepped onto the curb with the others.

Ms. Belfield flicked on the headlights of her Malibu, and veered to the right corner, continuing down the street into the dusk.

CHAPTER 23

TUESDAY AFTERNOON, 4:55 P.M.

Nipping her lower lip, Suellen peered out at the dark, dismal street. Her eyes swerved from side to side, searching for headlights. But the entire block was empty and drained of life, leaving only a sensation of death in its place.

Nothing like a serial killer to turn the neighborhood into a ghost town, she thought, feeling vulnerable.

She turned away and noticed the novel they were reading in school lying next to her on the cushioned window bench. This was normally a spot where she would read, or just lay out to unwind, let go of everything, and be to herself. But now, with the sheer terror that gripped her so, she was grateful not to be alone.

"Still no sign of Dad?" her brother asked. He was out of her view, sitting by the table in the dining room, a large space just past the stairway before the kitchen.

She sighed. "Not yet. I wish I had told him everything this morning. If I had, there's no way he would've even bothered going into work."

"At least your dad's not that far off," Brandon mentioned, sitting next to Slim on the sofa. "The way it's looking outside, my mom's probably going to have a tough time making it back home from Chicago tonight. Is it still coming down out there?"

"Yeah, harder than it was earlier," Suellen said glumly. "It's basically raining ice out there. I just hope Dad makes it home okay."

"I'm sure he will," Slim assured her. "It's us I'm worried about. I don't think I can sleep until all this is over with. Every time I close my eyes, I see us in that building…. being buried alive." Sitting with her hands placed inside her jean jacket, she shook her leg uncontrollably. She stared at the television, but was inattentive towards it. The glare of the screen reflected on her expressionless face.

"I know it was stupid of me to want to go in there," Brandon admitted. "But… I mean… I thought someone needed help. I couldn't just leave them there alone and scared. I didn't know it was just an old recording going off. If I had… I never would've…"

"Just forget about it," Slim muttered. "Nothing we can do about it now. I just hope he doesn't figure out that we were there. Because of us the police know he's here. I don't even want to imagine what he'll do if he learns we found out he's killed more people than they know about."

The room was invaded by a tense moment of silence so heavy and thick it nearly made the air hard to breathe. Turning away, Suellen faced the window but didn't stare out.

She cast her eyes down and dragged out a heavy, exasperated sigh that seemed to spread through the room and make the air even thicker. Suellen didn't know how to process all they had discovered. It overwhelmed her to a level of fear she had never experienced in her young life. There was no denying Sanderson had returned to the funeral home after the police searched it. In her mind, she saw the photos he had taken of them that night and wondered how long it had been since he'd been there. A few hours? Had they just missed him?

She looked over at everyone. They were still sulking.

Rubbing her forehead, Suellen let her eyes drift back on the floor. The woman's scream blaring in her memory was starting to give her a headache. Or maybe she just needed to eat. But as bad as she felt, she knew her body wouldn't allow anything to stay down. She spun her head up, hoping to spot her father's car rolling up the driveway.

What's taking him so long to get back? She wondered, growing concerned. She then remembered the slick road conditions and allowed herself to relax a bit. *He'll be back soon.*

Before another thought entered her mind, the phone rang. It seemed to blast through the quiet room as loudly as a train horn.

Andre stood from his chair and headed to the kitchen for the handset.

"That's probably Dad calling," Suellen said, feeling relieved. "I still don't know exactly how I'm going to tell him. But I just need to tell it like it is. And whatever happens, happens."

"You know we got your back, Su," Brandon assured her.

Moving from her spot by the window she gave a weak smile, then proceeded on to the kitchen with her brother. She saw him sitting sideways in a chair near the table in the center of the room. His right arm dangled over the top back end while he held the phone with the other hand.

He was so immersed in the conversation with the caller, he hadn't noticed his sister's sudden appearance until she was close enough for him to feel her presence. When he turned his head sharply towards her, his mouth hung open. The wide, distressed eyes he flashed petrified her to a standstill.

"What's wrong? What happened?" She asked in a loud whisper.

With the phone gripped in his hand, Andre shook his head. "You have no idea how bad this has all gotten."

CHAPTER 24

Gathered around the wide-screen, no one spoke a sound as they intently watched the news broadcast. Standing from the sofa, Slim stepped closer to the television near Suellen and Andre, who stood side by side. The broadcast continued on for what seemed like hours, showing footage of wrecked vehicles, and news anchors reporting on what had occurred.

Until it was finally cut off to a commercial break.

"Well this day just keeps getting better and better," Brandon muttered. Sitting on the tip end of the sofa he leaned forward, his hands pressed into firm fists resting on his knees.

"What else did Dad say?" Suellen asked, staring down at her brother.

Still holding the handset, Andre bent the small antenna back and forth with his thumb. "Just that he spoke to Miss Dowell and Mrs. Morrison. They weren't involved in the accident. But traffic is so backed up, they don't know how long it'll be before they can get back."

Slim placed a hand over her chest and felt the swift beat of her heart. "I just thank God they're alright."

"Did you tell Dad about what's going on?" Suellen asked.

"I didn't get the chance. He loaded me with so much news about how bad the weather's supposed to get. Then I think the call dropped. He said he'd be here as fast as he can. But the roads are real slick."

"This is just ridiculous," Brandon remarked, massaging the back of his neck.

"We can't lose it right now," said Suellen. "All we can do is— "

"Can't lose it!" Brandon exclaimed. "My mom was nearly involved in a thirty-car pile-up on Lake Shore Drive. And we're sitting here alone being stalked by a screwball serial killer who wants us dead! So please forgive me if I'm not exactly in cool, calm, and collected mood right now!"

"I get that you're angry. No one can blame you for that," Suellen replied in a comforting manner.

"But you can blame me for getting us in this mess to begin with. All of you do." He looked grim and angry.

"Whoa, all that doesn't even matter, Brandon," Andre started.

Brandon, lost in his own guilt, blocked out everything around him and went into an uncontrolled rant. "And why shouldn't you blame me? I do. If it weren't for me wanting to go out and commit a misdemeanor, none of this would have happened."

Avoiding eye contact, he stormed off into the kitchen and sat by the table with his back turned and head propped up against his hand.

He needed to be alone for the time being.

***

When Suellen opened her eyes sometime later that evening, she was uncertain where she was. She wiped her dreary eyes and rose to a sitting position on the cushioned window bench.

I don't even remember falling asleep, she thought.

After gazing around the brightly lit room, she recognized the living room. But something about it looked different. The television was now turned off, and everything else was as it should be. But something just didn't feel right. She somehow felt that something had happened while she slept.

"Andre?" she called out in trepidation. "Did Dad make it back?" He didn't answer.

"Andre? Slim? Brandon?" Still no response. It was as if she was all alone in the world.

"Dad— Andre," She called out louder. But immediately regretted doing so when the only sound she heard was the ringing in her ears.

She had never been so frightened by silence in all her life. Her eyes darted around the room as she carefully listened for the slightest response, but still heard nothing.

Her initial suspicions were now confirmed. *Something's not right! They wouldn't just leave like this! Something's wrong!*

She observed the curving stairway, half expecting her father, brother, or even one of her friends to step down. But the terror she felt contradicted her hopes.

I don't know what happened, all I know is I need to leave. Now!

Suellen jumped off the window bench to rush to the front door, but never made it that far.

Holding her breath, her body chilled when she saw blood leaking out from under the closet door, collecting into a growing pool on the hardwood floor. Stamped down in the puddle of blood was a large boot print that trailed down the floor and continued on into the kitchen.

Before Suellen could react, a hand emerged from behind her, pulling her back, and constricting her neck. Terror rushed to her heart as she fretfully made several desperate efforts to peel the cold hand from around her neck.

She gagged incessantly, feeling weaker with each second from the firm grasp that throttled her.

Tears began to form in the corners of her eyes as she knew she was confined within the unyielding grasp of death.

CHAPTER 25

Firmer and firmer the hand locked around her throat. She felt her breath trapped and tried squirming out the stern grasp. But the strangling left her body paralyzed.

Suellen swiveled her eyes at the front door that seemed to mock her. The fact that she was so close to freedom yet so helpless at the same time tore her down even more.

Her despairing gags for breath were lessoning by the second. The only thought Suellen had now was how much longer she had to suffer.

But as her body grew frailer, she feared she couldn't bear it much longer.

***

Suellen's eyes shot open and she leaped off the bed. Disoriented, she wiped away the cold sweat that drenched her face and stared around. She had never been so relieved to be safe in her bedroom.

Panting robustly, she rubbed a hand across her neck, just to be convinced nothing was there. The horrid sensation of the cold, strapping hand still lingered, the entire nightmare pinned to her memory, refusing to die.

She placed a hand over her chest, feeling her heart accelerate like a swift drumbeat. Her right arm started tingling. And although she knew it had just fallen asleep, she had to look down at it, just to be assured she wasn't being grabbed.

"I'm okay," Suellen sighed, shaking her arm, "it was just a dre—nightmare. A horrible, horrible nightmare."

But it felt so....so real. Suellen realized, struck by a deep affliction.

Staring through her dark room, her eyes landed on the open doorway. Brightness from the tall lamp out in the hall poured inside, illuminating the entrance in a square of light.

I swear I could feel everything that was happening. As if I was really being choked. She positioned herself at the edge of the bed. Shutting her eyes and reopening them. Wishing she could separate herself from her frightening thoughts. But the nightmare kept replaying in her mind.

But what if it was real? What would I have done then? Would Sanderson have killed me?

A shrill whistle caught her attention.

I meant to close that window earlier, she thought, feeling the cold breeze. The curtains fluttered from the soft draft that seeped in through the small opening.

Suellen flinched at the sudden brightness that penetrated her bedroom. When she saw her father leaning on the doorframe, still in his uniform pants and white undershirt, she nearly ran over to him, wrapping her arms around his waist.

"Hey there, sleepy Su. Thought you might be out for the rest of the night. It's almost eleven-thirty." As she loosened her hug, he put his arm around her shoulder.

"I didn't even know I was sleep. Just came in here to lay down and must have dozed off. I must have been more tired than I realized to sleep in my school clothes."

"That's understandable. As I've been told you all have had quite an escapade these past few days."

She could feel him staring down at her. In her mind, she searched for words to say, but was rendered speechless. For what seemed like so long Suellen had wanted to tell her father all that had happened. She imagined how he might react to the news, but never once thought of how she would respond.

"Are you mad?" Suellen stared at his face as he frowned down on her.

"That none of you all told your parents right off the bat that your lives were in danger? Being mad is an understatement. Did you not understand the severity of this? This guy is an escaped murderer, not to mention an arsonist. To not say anything is practically suicide. You all are old enough to know better."

"I know, Dad, but we really didn't think it was that serious at first." She fought back tears. It was hard for her to believe so much had changed, so much had transpired in a matter of three days.

Her father paused and held her closer. "Well, the police were here earlier. Andre, Sabrina, and Brandon told them everything, even about him having his car painted. And the recording you all heard today. But with the weather the way it is, there's not much they can do at the moment other than put out an all-points bulletin. It's terrible out there.

"Your friends have to stay here until their parents can make it back. They managed to get to a warming center downtown. Ice is sticking to everything and it's still coming down. Even with the salt trucks out. I had to take my time driving home. And the falling temperatures on top of all this aren't going to make it any better."

"So do you think he left then?" Suellen asked, arching her head up towards him.

"Police didn't exactly say that when I spoke to them, but with this ice storm they don't believe we have to worry about him showing up. As far as my professional opinion, that's just a tactic to put our minds at ease. They do have an officer canvassing the area however.

"But I assure you all, with me around, this coward won't be breathing the same air as you. He'll barely be breathing at all if I really have my way with him."

All the terror Suellen had experienced just moments ago was starting to melt away by her father's consoling words.

"I spoke with Mom today. Granddad's surgery went fine. She'll be on the next available flight to O'Hare. Which will hopefully be tomorrow sometime."

"I hope so too," Suellen replied. "Feels like she's been gone a month. It hasn't even been a week yet."

"She'll be back soon. And by the time she is, this whole ordeal will be blown over. School is already cancelled tomorrow. And I doubt it'll be open the rest of the week, so rest up. Sabrina's asleep in the guest room and Brandon's got the air mattress in the room with Andre. There's nothing to worry about. I made some turkey burgers and cut up some fries for everyone. There's still some left if you're hungry."

Suellen covered her mouth while she let out a long-winded yawn. "Think I'm just going back to sleep."

Charles bent over and kissed his daughter on the forehead.

"Glad my friends didn't see that," she teased, with a playfully crinkled face.

He chuckled, rubbed the top of her head, and sauntered off into the hall.

Feeling refreshed and rid of all troubles, Suellen began humming blissfully. She still remained a bit uneasy knowing Sanderson was still at large. But she felt confident and assured he wouldn't be harassing them anymore.

After closing the door almost all the way, she went over to the dresser to pull out her bed clothes. A fast-paced buzz surfaced in the room, and she stopped midway to the dresser.

She gazed at the small opening in the window and realized a strong blast of air was rattling the bottom of the blinds, creating the drone sound. She went to flick the light off, then hurried over to the window. Once she pushed it shut, she observed through the flakes of frost on the glass to the scenery outside.

The branches from the tree right outside were layered with a thin coating of ice. And although the window was closed now, cold air still trickled in. She heard the sound of rustling, and looked down.

A bunch of dry leaves whirled at the side of the house like a tornado. They swirled for only seconds longer before being carried off into the night.

After a final glance, Suellen moved from the window and strolled across the room. She turned the light back on then proceeded to her dresser, her mind set on getting a much-needed, restful slumber.

She stared at her dark reflection in the oval mirror perched on top of her dresser. Her pink undershirt was wrinkled and her hair was disheveled from her restless sleep. She snatched hold of the blue bandanna that lay on her dresser and tied it around the top of her head.

She saw a flash from her dream of her being choked and shook it from her mind.

As she searched the drawer for bed clothes, she prayed to God her nightmare wouldn't come to pass while she slept through the blustery night hours.

CHAPTER 26

WEDNESDAY MORNING, 8:32 A.M.

Tap tap tap tap. The falling sleet battered the unmarked police car as the officer travelled at a steady pace. He passed by many vehicles draped with dense ice, parked alongside the curb.

Although no one else was out driving, the salt trucks' inability to keep up with the rapid build-up of ice made for slick conditions.

With his wipers on high, the officer rolled through a stop sign as he made a right turn. His headlights beamed onto a red Oldsmobile parked at the side of the road further down at the end of the block. He pulled over behind it and slowed to a stop.

"This looks like our guy," he muttered, rising from his seat and approaching the Oldsmobile. Tiny pellets of ice bounced and landed on top of his shaved head.

The officer placed a hand on his holstered pistol while proceeding with vigilant steps on the ice. He pulled a flashlight out and shined it forward. The door on the driver's side was gaping wide open, but the vehicle had been abandoned.

With his suspicions confirmed, he called in for backup. "This is Officer Caldwell. I have located suspect's vehicle at the corner of Jackson and Mort. Suspect might be in the vicinity. Please send out back-up to three forty-seven Mort Road. I repeat, send back-up to three forty-seven Mort Road. Over."

Caldwell waited for a response but heard only static. "Do you copy? Again this is Officer Cald—"

Before he could continue, he suffered a brutal strike to the back of the head and went sprawling to the ground. He let out a heavy grunt as he rolled over onto his back, and stared at his assailant standing over him. His eyes flared with anger through the ski mask.

Before the policeman even had a chance to reach for his weapon, Sanderson struck him twice more in the head, knocking him out cold.

With a large tire iron propped over his shoulder, Sanderson stared down at the motionless officer and shook his head with mock sympathy. "To serve and protect," he said in a low snooty manner. "Can't even take a blow to the back of the head. Such a disgrace to that badge."

He then went to his own car and threw the heavy object down on the driver's seat. Before leaning back out, he pressed a button near the steering wheel under the dashboard that popped the trunk open.

Afterwards, he returned to Officer Caldwell and with little effort hurled him over a shoulder. Fresh blood trickled down his victim's head. Sanderson carried the limp body to the trunk, and rolled him in.

The radio on Caldwell crackled as one of his colleagues attempted to reach him. But the signal was so bad, only static came through. For a moment, Sanderson glared down at the fallen man.

He snatched up the officer's radio and gun, then slammed the trunk shut and moseyed off as if nothing had happened. Tossing the two items in the sewer drain at the side of the curb.

CHAPTER 27

WEDNESDAY MORNING, 10:06 A.M.

The incessant steady rhythm of sleet falling onto the house awakened Suellen from her soothing slumber. She turned over onto her back and stretched out across the bed. Clearing her throat, she then sat up in bed and eyed her room cautiously. She half expected to spot bloody footprints on the floor. But after seeing nothing peculiar, she pulled her small head scarf off and started out of bed.

I've got to stop thinking about that dream.

Suellen stood by her bed and stretched with a yawn. Although the material of her plaid pink and black flannel lounge pants were made thin, she felt quite warm. The air was heavy and thick and she fanned her chest with her dark brown shirt.

"Dad must have turned the heat all the way up."

Suellen eyed the doorway and looked directly out into the hall. She could hear the faint sound of the television downstairs as she went to shut the door.

Didn't I close this door last night? She wondered.

Not giving it another thought, her mind went to her stomach as she realized she hadn't eaten anything at all yesterday. She just didn't have an appetite, but now hunger was calling her.

Suellen rushed over to the closet to pick out a pair of old jeans she could wear around the house. The idea of going downstairs to prepare herself some breakfast made her move even faster. She had a taste for cereal.

***

Sitting at the kitchen table finishing off her second bowl of Honey Nut Cheerios, Suellen looked up periodically, watching Brandon. He sat on the arm of the sofa, his eyes unmoving from the televised news report on the ice storm.

She had greeted him on her way to the kitchen and he'd responded, but still remained distant. And although he didn't appear to be angry anymore, his mood was a bit standoffish, like he didn't want to be bothered with anyone at the moment.

He still feels guilty. Thinks it's all his fault.

Suellen got up from the chair to dump her bowl into the sink, then turned and made her way into the living room to join Brandon.

He hadn't moved from his spot. The right leg of his blue jogging pants was raised to his knee as he pulled the string of his matching hooded sweatshirt
back and forth.

"Feels weird not being at school in the middle of the day," said Suellen, taking a seat beside him. "So what are they saying about this storm? Sounds like the sleet has stopped out there."

"Yeah but it came down just about all night. Now they're saying it's supposed to drop even more. We're already at twenty below, and that's without the wind chill."

"It's far from twenty below in here," Slim remarked as she came down the stairs. She wore the same khakis and sweater from the day before. From the top of the stairs, Andre followed after her. He held onto the railing to prevent a fall from his jeans, which were a bit long for him.

Suellen moved and headed towards the dining room where the thermostat was. She had intended to turn the heat down earlier but it slipped her mind.

Fixing her eyes on the digital thermostat, she gasped. "No wonder it's burning up, this thing's up at one thirty!"

"One thirty?" Her brother repeated, watching his sister from the entryway. "Why'd Dad turn it up so high? He never does that."

Suellen pressed a lower button on the thermostat until she brought it down to 80, then faced her brother and shrugged. "I don't know. Maybe he wanted to warm the whole house up since it's so cold out, but forgot to turn it back down. He's probably still in bed sle—."

A soft brittle crackle coming from somewhere nearby cut her off.

Slim threw her head over a shoulder. "What was that?"

Suellen and Andre rushed over to the window at the end of the dining room table.

The outer glass was shielded with a sheet of ice, making it difficult to see out. The only thing they could halfway recognize was the tree at the side of the house.

Struck with a sense of confusion, Andre left the window and joined the others by the couch. His sister stayed behind. Leaning her back against the wall she crossed her arms tightly over her chest.

"I don't know what that was. But from what I could see, nobody's out there," she stated.

"It sounded like something broke apart," said Andre, scratching the back of his neck before he lowered himself into the lounge chair.

"Or something shattering," Slim added, sitting next to Brandon. "That cop is still watching the area, right?"

"He has to be," Andre assured her. "They said he's supposed to call and send somebody out if anything happens."

With her eyes down, Slim stared at the smooth wooden floor until her vision was blurred. "I know. I don't know why I'm so jumpy. We told the police everything and they're doing their jobs. But this is so unreal. We don't have serial killers around here. I just can't wait for all this to be over." She pulled a hair band off her wrist and tied her hair back with it.

"It will be soon," Suellen proclaimed. She had left the dining room and was now making her way over toward the chair her brother occupied.

"I never meant for any of this to happen," Brandon blurted out.

"Stop blaming yourself, Brandon," said Slim. "The only one at fault here is the fugitive on the run. Let's just be grateful we're all okay and he didn't get a chance to hurt us."

Giving her direct eye contact, Brandon flashed Slim a weak grin. "Thanks. I'm just ready for them to catch this guy already. I slept okay, better than I expected but I'm still kind of drowsy. Those winds were high last night. Had me up most of the night."

"They still are high," Andre remarked, glancing back over to the window. His arms folded across his chest.

Suellen was the only one standing. She looked over at everyone and after noticing how weary and on edge they still were, she quickly decided not to tell them about the dream she'd had.

We're already living a nightmare, no need to share mine.

"Anybody watching this?" Brandon asked as he reached for the remote.

"You can see what else is on," Suellen told him, turning to her brother. "I'm going to give Ma a call. See how she's doing and when her flight should arrive."

Unfolding his arms, Andre raised his body in the chair. "I want to talk to her when you're done."

Together they went into the kitchen as their guests began to search the channels.

Suellen grabbed the phone off the countertop, while her brother continued over to the right and pulled out a bowl for cereal from the above cabinet.

"Can you turn that coffee pot off, Andre? I put that on for Dad earlier but forgot about it. I thought he'd be up by now, but he's probably worn out."

After flicking the pot off and unplugging it, Andre circled his gaze around the kitchen. "Do you hear that?"

"Hear what?"

Without answering, he surveyed the room with his eyes once more, viewing the powder blue countertop with the matching above and below cabinets that wrapped around the right side of the kitchen.

"I think it just stopped. It sounded like a low scream." Andre kept looking around for the source of the subtle noise he had heard when he noticed the basement door was half open. He spun to face his sister, who noticed it also.

"That door was closed earlier. Maybe Dad's down there doing laundry," she hoped, holding the cordless phone with a tight grip. Without looking, she set it back down on the counter near its charger.

"Yeah maybe," Andre said, feeling strangely doubtful. "But we were right in the other room. He wouldn't have not said anything, or left the coffee pot on."

Andre gradually edged his way closer to the basement door. From outside, rough, cold winds blew noisily against the house. He went on only two steps more before Suellen grabbed his arm and jerked him back towards her.

"Something's happened," she whispered. "Look at the doorknob."

Right away he lowered his eyes to the knob on the basement door and stared at the heavy red smear that covered it.

CHAPTER 28

"No way! He can't be here!" His low voice began to quiver as his face lined with sheer terror. "How could he be? The police were supposed to call us if— "

Suellen threw a hand over his mouth. "We don't have time to figure out how he got in."

She promptly went for the phone again. But made no attempt to grab it after realizing the wire connecting the charger to the wall had been cut.

Suellen and Andre faced the basement doorway and squinted into the darkness that lay on the other side. All the comfort they had ever felt in their home had now shifted to great trepidation.

In a dash, Suellen entered the other room, pulling Andre behind her. "Follow us! Hurry!" She told Slim and Brandon. They quickly moved from the sofa and trailed after Suellen and Andre up the stairs, hopping two and three steps at once.

"Is everything okay?" Slim had questioned.

Suellen made certain not to respond until reaching the very top. And even then, she spoke softly as she hurried down the hall to her parents' room. "Sanderson's here. He's inside."

"Say what now?!" Brandon shouted.

"Are you sure?" Slim asked, gaping down the stairs.

"Positive," replied Andre, panting. "He cut the phone cords!"

Leading the way, Suellen took a pause to face everyone. "SSHHHH! Listen, he's in the house. Or he was. I don't know. But he got in. As soon as we get our dad we're all outta here."

They kept down the hall at a fast pace the short distance to Charles' room.

Within seconds, Suellen turned the handle on the door and swung it open, flicking the light switch on as they entered. But Charles wasn't inside.

As they all entered the master bedroom, it became obvious that a struggle had occurred. Several papers that were once stacked on Mrs. Blanchard's work desk were now cluttered on the floor. On the opposite end of the room were the heavy covers that lay in a heap on the bedside.

"Dad?" Andre called out, praying for a response.

"Dad?" Suellen echoed. But the only sound that came was the crackling noise outside again.

"He's not here," Brandon told them, unable to look up from the littered floor. "Sanderson must have him."

This can't be happening. This can't be happening. Suellen repeated to herself. She was starting to feel the very same terror from the night before that she'd felt in her dream. She wanted so badly for this whole ordeal to be a horrible dream. And to wake up from this nightmare at any second. But it was now a reality for them all. She fought back tears accepting the fact that all of this was real. Deadly real.

Suellen glanced at her brother, who still had his gaze glued to the floor.

"It'll be okay. We'll find him." Slim said comfortingly, seeing how distressed they were.

As they inched further into the room, Suellen focused on their family portrait sitting on her mother's dresser. Even from a distance, she could make out their happy smiles in the photo.

Just above the wide dresser was a large round mirror that hung against the wall near the far right corner of the room. Reflected in the mirror was the unmade bed and more covers that had fallen onto the floor.

Next to the blanket was a small pool of fresh blood that had spilled over and ran under the bed. Written in the middle of the blood puddle was a message that read, NIGHT GHOST STRIKES.

CHAPTER 29

At first sight, no one could move or speak. From outside, another crackling sound arose. This one was more intense than before and came with a splitting rattle at the end. But no one paid it any mind.

Suellen gazed down at the blood, wondering how she could have been deaf to the chaos that must have transpired in the room adjacent to hers. Just the thought of her father being attacked battered her like a blow in the gut. Her chest throbbed, but her body was stiff as a corpse.

Andre began to approach the horror scene. Slim and Brandon started to follow, but hesitated and stopped before reaching the bed. Andre kneeled down to the floor and looked under the bed, then quickly stood up again. "He's not here. He must have him somewhere else."

"We can't stay here," said Brandon, talking fast. "We need to get next door to a neighbor's and notify the cops. When they get here they'll find Mr. Blanchard and he'll be okay. But there's no time now."

With no objections, Suellen and Andre followed Brandon and Slim out the room.

They had nearly reached the stairwell when Suellen suddenly felt faint. Knowing that her father was somewhere hurt and then abandoning him was really getting the best of her. It took all her strength to hold it together to keep from breaking down.

With the front door now in view, they practically ran down the stairs.

"We're almost out!" Brandon shouted.

Then, just as he was about to hop off the final step, a tall man, wearing wrinkled jeans and a dingy hooded sweatshirt, approached the bottom of the stairs. In his hand was a large tire iron.

Brandon grabbed hold of the banister and stopped abruptly, causing the others to bump into him. Brandon stared into the intruder's cold, hard eyes for the first time.

He looked different from his mug shot in the newspaper. His dark beard was thick and scruffy, and a cut on his forehead was covered up with a small bandage. His glare moved from Brandon, and on up to Slim, Andre, and then settled on Suellen. Who immediately averted her eyes, and focused on the several gray and white patterns that made up his hooded sweatshirt.

"Well, well, well, it's nice to finally meet you all face to face," Sanderson said. He spoke with a southern accent. His voice was gruff and intimidating. "Seems like we're old friends."

"Oh God!" Slim exclaimed, noticing the pistol stuffed into the side of his pants.

Sanderson followed her stare, then looked up at her and smiled menacingly. "That's just my little persuader, as I call it. Always gets the job done. One way or another." He advanced on them. And with a swift move, grabbed Brandon's wrist and yanked him down.

Brandon frantically attempted to free himself from the strong grip but was unsuccessful. "You better let go, old man!"

With a burst of fury, Sanderson threw Brandon violently against the wall. "You might wanna watch it with the name calling, young blood. Mind me now. This old man can hurt more than just your feelings."

Sanderson shifted his attention to Slim, Andre, and Suellen, who remained on the stairway, much too terrified to move an inch. He pointed the tire iron at them. "Into the kitchen. NOW!"

They followed his orders and began walking. Sanderson started right after them, half dragging an aching Brandon along by the wrist.

"Come on, young blood, shake it off! That wasn't nearly as bad as getting hit by a car would've been! Don't you think?"

Brandon groaned, massaging his forehead.

"Hey, Little Miss Brunette," Sanderson called, referring to Slim. "Go over to the thermostat and turn it all the way up. Like I had it earlier. And don't be getting any slick ideas. You wouldn't want your friends here to come up second best in a battle with a tire iron. Would you? And keep my little persuader in mind as well. You can't outrun a bullet. Trust me."

Slim immediately did as she was told.

Andre turned sharply around and stepped up to Sanderson. "What have you done with my dad?"

"Andre don't!" his sister shouted through a whisper.

The prowler narrowed his eyes at Andre. "You shouldn't be concerned over matters that are out of your control."

What does that mean! Suellen wondered. Several questions raced through her mind all at once. *How long has he been in here? Did he kill our father! And what is he going to do with us!*

Slim had returned from the other room without uttering a word. But her large eyes revealed much nervousness.

"Now keep going! All of you."

The girls continued on, but Andre stood his ground, staring into the assailant's daunting grimace.

Sanderson's expression hardened and he lowered himself to his challenger. "Not telling you twice, tough guy. Do you need some persuasion to get you going?"

Andre stared him down for only seconds longer before proceeding to the kitchen. As he walked through the doorway, Sanderson shoved him over to the right with his weapon.

"You three. By the counter. Don't even think of moving!"

On the far end of the room by the open basement door was a large red gasoline can. There was no wondering what his intentions were now. Just the thought of being set on fire made Suellen grip the counter, her mind raided with rigid tension.

The fugitive turned to Brandon and gradually released his wrist. "Alright, buddy boy, you look like you've bounced back. Go over to that table and bring four chairs this way in the middle of the floor. Line them up side by side!"

"For what?" Brandon demanded his face tight with anger.

"It's not for musical chairs, that's for sure." Sanderson let out a deep, low chuckle that seemed to echo throughout the quiet house. "I need to teach you morons a lesson about the dangers of late night excursions. You brought this on yourselves you know! All I wanted was to lay low in this here town for a few days. Catch up on some much needed rest and be on my way out. But instead I end up having to dodge the police. And losing what little belongings and prized possessions I had. All because you four practically led the cops to where I was on your little expedition!"

"But we didn't know," Slim cried.

"The things you all don't know could fill up a whole new world." He rasped. "But don't sweat it. I've already figured everything out. And the way I have it planned, looks like curiosity won't be the only thing that kills you!"

Brandon glared at the intruder. His hands squeezed into tight fists at his side. Sanderson displayed a spiteful smirk, as if pleased with himself for making them feel so threatened. He calmly strolled over and stood right in front of Suellen, though he faced the opposite direction, watching Brandon carry the first chair over.

"HURRY UP!" he shouted, swinging the tire iron with such force it whistled through the air. "You can move more than one chair at a time! There's really no sense in stalling!"

Still taking his time, Brandon went for two more chairs. Suellen shifted her gaze off Brandon and saw thick balls of rope hanging out Sanderson's two back pockets. The fretful thudding of her heartbeat felt like it was soaring to her throat. There was no denying the fact that he meant to kill them.

Feeling trapped and miserable, she shot her eyes around the room, looking for something, anything to fend off their assailant long enough for them to escape. She whiffed the aroma of brewed coffee and brought her attention to the coffee pot, still sitting inside the maker, with steam floating from the carafe.

With a trembling hand, Suellen reached for the pot, and waited. *Just one good splash in the face should be enough for us to run out the back door.* Slim and Andre quickly caught on to the plan and helped her lookout.

"Took you long enough," the man complained as Brandon finished his task. "Doesn't matter, though. Now the fun really begins!" He cackled for a moment, as if he'd made some kind of inside joke that only he understood. "Night Ghost strikes again! And again! And again! And again!"

Suellen held the pot handle tighter, scared it might slip from her grasp. Her throat grew dry and her legs shook with discomfort. She knew there was only one chance at this. And no room for error.

Sanderson peered over his shoulder. And in that instant, Suellen threw the hot coffee directly in his face. He arched back with a deafening holler that filled the room as the tire iron fell from his hand.

On an impulse, she swung the coffee pot at him, striking Sanderson dead in the jaw. Shards of glass went flying across the kitchen.

"RUN!" Suellen screamed. But she and the others were already fleeing to the back door. Before Suellen got too far away, a hand clasped her shoulder and hurled her back onto the floor. She looked up to see

Sanderson standing above her, facing Andre, Slim, and Brandon as they neared the door.

    Without as much as a word he pulled out his pistol, aimed it, and fired three shots at them.

CHAPTER 30

Glass shattered as he fired blindly, unknowingly missing his targets who had ducked low at the sound of the first shot.

Suellen nearly jumped out her skin from the explosion. It was so much louder than she ever anticipated. Even afterwards, the sound of the gunshots remained in her ears.

Sanderson rotated around to Suellen. His left jaw was a mixture of blood and coffee that rolled through his beard and dripped from his now reddened face. But the defiant stare he threw down at her was unmoving. "It's always the quiet ones you got to look out for," he rasped through gritted teeth. "You little idiot! You don't even know how big a mistake you just made!"

He aimed the gun at her now, making her cringe.

"On your feet!" He demanded.

But before she could get up, Andre emerged and tackled Sanderson from the side. The gun flew from his grip and slid across the floor along with them. Andre jumped to his feet and went to help his sister up.

When Sanderson climbed up, Slim and Brandon drove the round table toward him, ramming him against the wall. But their attacker pushed back harder and sent them crashing to the floor. Suellen and Andre ran to their aid.

When they looked back up, Sanderson had the tire iron raised in the air, ready to swing.

"Who would have ever thought four little helpless whelps could cause me so much trouble," he remarked, chilling menace in his voice.

They circled the floor, staying on the opposite end of Sanderson as he attempted to near them. Brandon stood out front, while the others watched from behind. Sanderson lunged forward after them. Brandon quickly snatched up a large piece of broken glass from the coffee pot and held it out defensively in a trembling hand.

"Back off before I slice up your other jaw, mister!" Brandon retorted.

Sanderson came to a stop and lowered his weapon. "Didn't your parents ever tell you not to play with sharp objects, young blood?" He questioned arrogantly. "Better put it down before you hurt yourself."

"You all run! Get outta here!" Brandon told the others.

But they were practically cornered on the far end of the kitchen, away from the back door and the entrance that led to the living room. The only exit near them they had a chance of getting to was the basement behind them.

Quickly Suellen, Slim, and Andre ran to their only route of escape and down the stairs. Staying behind, Brandon kept his weapon pointed at their intruder.

Sanderson shook his head. "You don't even know what to do with that. So just drop it, kid."

Brandon leaned forward and swiped his weapon through the air. His attacker suddenly grew enraged. Brandon jumped to the side as the tire iron came swinging over at him, just missing his head. He intentionally dropped the glass, grabbing up a nearby chair. He swung it at his opponent, grunting with each swipe.

Brandon struck him in the face once, then sent him diving to the floor, right on top of the gun. He threw the chair at the fugitive before darting away to the basement. The last thing he heard after shutting the door was a round of several gunshots as Sanderson fired at him.

***

With nothing but darkness surrounding him, terror clung to his muscles. Brandon stood still, halfway down the stairs leaning back against the banister, too afraid to make any sudden moves. His heart racing, he listened for imminent footsteps over his heavy panting, but heard only the wind gusting outside.

"Brandon. You okay!" Slim called to him from the dark at the bottom of the stairs where she waited with Suellen and Andre. Brandon hurried down the rest of the way to join them.

"I fought him off for as long as I could," he said, still catching his breath. "He's probably on his way down here! We need to find a way out now! This may be our last chance!"

"We can climb out over there," Suellen pointed down to the washer and dryer at the end of the room. Above them was one of the long windows at ground level near the basement ceiling.

They started over, but then froze at the sound of a long, low moan just ahead of them. Although it was soft and barely audible, Suellen recognized it and turned to her brother.

"It's Dad!" She whispered loudly.

CHAPTER 31

Suellen hurried back to the foot of the stairs and snatched up the flashlight from the tool chest. She flicked it on and pointed it straight in front of her. There, lying on his side in the middle of the floor, with his arms and legs bound tightly, was Mr. Blanchard, still wearing his uniform pants and white undershirt from last night.

Everyone rushed over to his rescue. Suellen bent down and pulled off the wide strip of duct tape that secured his mouth.

"There's no telling how long he's been down here," said Brandon. He stepped over behind Mr. Blanchard and started loosening the thick rope from his wrists, while Slim and Andre frantically worked to free his ankles.

Shining the flashlight on her father, Suellen saw a deep cut in his forehead. His head rested in a pool of his own blood that had slid down from the wound. Still unconscious, he moaned again as the ropes came off of him and they gently moved him over onto his back to slow the bleeding.

In a wild burst, Suellen thought of many different ways to get her father out of the house. But in the back of her mind she knew it was best they didn't move him anymore. They had no idea how long he had been down there. Or how badly he was injured. She briefly shut her eyes, hoping the damage done to her father wasn't life threatening.

"You better turn that off," Andre whispered to Suellen. "That lunatic could be down here at any second. He sees that thing on, he'll pop us all point blank."

Suellen gawked up the stairs to the closed basement door, watching it warily. "I don't even hear anything." She turned the flashlight off anyway.

"Maybe he left," Slim hoped, her voice nothing but a choked whisper.

"Wouldn't bet on it," Brandon remarked. "But we need to leave. Get next door or something so we can call the cops and get an ambulance out here."

Something thumped from overhead. They listened, and heard it again seconds later.

"Someone's at the front door," Andre stated.

"Chief Blanchard? It's the police," the officer addressed loudly in a deep assertive voice.

Suellen and the others briefly stood in stunned silence before rocketing up the stairs to the front door.

There's no way he's still here with the cops right outside! Suellen figured. Relief rushed to her heart as she swung the basement door open.

As soon as she stepped into the disarranged kitchen, she covered her nose. A strong odor had invaded the room. It was almost unbearable.

"It's gas," Slim stated, wrapping an arm around her face.

There was another hard knock on the front door. "Chief Blanchard. Are you in there? Police."

Ignoring the smell, they trounced over the broken glass, past the overturned chairs, and continued to the living room.

"Not so fast!" Sanderson said in a hushed voice. He crept up behind them and snatched Slim and Brandon before they could make it through the doorway. He had removed his leather jacket, revealing a long spider web tattoo on his left arm that wrapped around like a snake. With his strapping arms, he held them both aggressively in a headlock. Suellen and Andre watched helplessly from the other room as Slim and Brandon failed at every attempt to break free.

"Now listen up," Sanderson demanded, his voice a daunting whisper. "There's gasoline all over this kitchen. If that cop isn't gone in five minutes, I got a lighter in my pocket that can send your two friends here up in flames."

The officer knocked again. "Anyone home? It's the police."

Sanderson cut his gaze to the door then back on his victims. "One of you had better get that," Sanderson told Suellen and Andre, who stood unmoving, grounded by terror. "Just remember, five minutes. One false move, and you're all dead."

They watched as he tightened the hold on his victims' throats and rounded the corner back into the kitchen.

CHAPTER 32

The doorbell chimed repeatedly, followed by several hard knocks. With trembling legs Suellen made her way to the door. Doing her best to put on a look of contentment, she wiped her tear-filled eyes and took a deep breath before swinging the door open.

The officer stared down at her. His stern pale face was starting to turn red from the cold. "Good morning, young lady. I'm sorry to wake you if you were asleep. But is everything okay?"

"Yeah we're fine," she answered a little too quickly.

"Is your father in?"

"No. I mean— yeah. He's upstairs sleep." She looked off to the side, careful not to reveal her apprehension through eye contact. But the officer leaned over, trying to see her face. Feeling compelled, she turned her head to him, but quickly averted her eyes.

A cold draft blew inside, making her shiver even more.

"Do you think your dad would mind if I came in for a minute? It's a little nippy out here and I have some questions I'd like to ask."

"Uh, I guess not," Suellen said with a rising heart rate. She reluctantly stepped aside, urgently trying to conjure a way to inform him of the peril they were in without being too obvious. But her thoughts were crammed with nerves.

The officer strolled in, giving the room a quick scan while he stood by the stairway.

"Hey there, little man," he greeted Andre, who stood a distance away. Hands jammed into his pockets.

"We t-t-told you e-e-everything we know," Andre stammered, joining his sister by the front door.

"I don't believe we met when I came over before," the policeman said to Suellen as he surveyed the room again. "I'm Officer Thompson. I came by yesterday evening to get your statements about your encounters with the fugitive Albert Sanderson. As I'm sure you're aware, he's an extremely dangerous man and I can assure you, we're doing everything in our power to capture him.

"My colleague is checking in with the officer that's canvassing the area as we speak. But I'm actually here responding to a disturbance call. One of your neighbors called in reportedly hearing gunshots from around here. Have any of you heard any suspicious noises?"

Leaning against the wall, Andre just shook his head.

"Nope. I don't think so," Suellen replied, feeling her body grow hot as the temperature in the room soared.

The policeman looked back and forth at them. "Are you sure? Your neighbor sounded pretty convinced. Even mentioned how she heard glass shattering."

An exploding bang broke out from above. Suellen and Andre threw their focus up to the ceiling.

Did he put a bomb in the house?! Suellen thought

"Just the branches falling off from the tree outside," the officer said as if reading her mind. He watched them carefully. "It's happening all over town due to the heavy ice."

THUMP! THUD! THUMP! THUD! BAAAAAAANG! More tree limbs snapped off and hammered onto the roof, nearly rocking the house.

"M-Maybe that's what they heard then," Andre tried to convince him.

"Yeah, maybe," said Officer Thompson, noticing their agitated behavior. "Still doesn't explain the shatter your neighbor heard."

How long has he been in here? Suellen began to wonder. *Two minutes? Three? Four?* She could feel Sanderson growing suspicious of them from the other room.

The officer observed them again, then turned his gaze up the stairway. "Would it be possible to get your father down here? And your other two friends who were with you? So I can get their statements on the matter."

"No, I don't think so," Suellen replied, glancing away from the kitchen and at the officer. "They're all still sleep."

Thompson nodded with a narrow gaze. "I see. Well if there's nothing else, I guess I'll be on my way."

He placed a hand on his holster, and started towards the front door. "You kids have a good day now." Before they could respond, the officer leaned down and whispered to them, "I smelled the gas as soon as I walked in. He's in the kitchen, right?"

They nodded, feeling both relieved and yet still frightened.

"You gotta get our dad, too. He's in the basement," Suellen whispered back.

"Go to the back seat of the squad car. You'll be safe there." The officer began to step away, gradually moving in direction of the kitchen, pointing his gun down with both hands.

Just as Andre was set to open the door, Slim screamed from the other room.

"PLEEEEEASE! HELP US!"

CHAPTER 33

The policeman lunged forward into the kitchen, his Glock 22 pointed out ahead of him.

What happened? What did he do to them? Suellen shut her eyes, too afraid to go see for herself.

Slim and Brandon came darting through the doorway, stopping when they neared their two companions by the door.

"PUT YOUR HANDS UP AND SLOWLY MOVE TOWARDS ME!" Thompson ordered, aiming his gun straight out. "NOW!" The officer waited for only a short time before Sanderson appeared at the kitchen doorway. His arms raised high as he glared at the cop straight in the eye.

"Save that ugly stare for your mug shot," said the policeman. "Now turn around! Hands on your head!"

The fugitive cut his eyes upon the four adolescents, then obeyed the officer. "Might not want to pull that trigger, officer," Sanderson advised smugly. "Ironically it might not be the brightest idea."

"Thanks for the chemistry lesson, professor," Thompson replied harshly. He patted Sanderson down from shoulders to his ankles. "Where's the gun!"

"Look around on the floor and maybe you'll spot it if your eyes are still in function," Sanderson growled. "It's all fired out. Didn't think I would need that many."

Thompson quickly surveyed the kitchen and spotted the firearm. It lay on the floor under the round table.

"You kids can head on to the squad car," the policeman instructed, pulling out his handcuffs. "Don't worry. I've got this under control."

But before Thompson could bind him, Sanderson made a swift move and seized the gun. He reached for the officer's waist belt and snatched hold of his mace, spraying him in the face. The officer dropped to his knees hollering.

Sanderson aimed the gun down at him. His face took on a smirk as he watched the officer wipe at his eyes. Then he raised the gun and pointed it at the front door. "Any of you try to make a break for it I got a new round of bullets that won't mind following you! Now all of you, get over here!"

Brandon led the way as they slowly sauntered over. A cold breeze from the open door trailed them all the way.

"Don't do it! It's not worth it!" The policeman shouted, covering his eyes with both hands. "I've already alerted back-up. They're on their way. It's over, Sanderson!"

Sanderson cocked his head to the side, eyeballing the cop as if he'd offended him. "Perhaps you didn't get the memo. I'm running this show. And I'm currently not accepting applications for a new host. Sorry!"

Sanderson swung his arm low and shot the officer in the chest. He glared at the witnesses. His face was a twisted sneer. And his eyes were wild as he watched the four cringe with fear.

"You see that! You see what you made me do! YOU SEE WHAT YOU MADE ME DO!" Without realizing it, he dropped the can of mace.

Slim watched it roll over to the officer's inert body.

"You're murderers! All of you are murderers!" The intruder ranted hysterically, pacing the floor a few times before stopping. "You did that! Not me! It's your fault! YOUR FAULT!"

"Okay okay," Brandon said, his arms out in front as if to shield himself. He looked down to the gun at his side, then stared into the deranged man's face.

They weren't even sure if he was looking at them, or somewhere else in his head. The only thing about him they were certain of was if they attempted to get away, he'd shoot them all.

Suellen pulled Andre back towards her. And placed a hand across his chest, feeling his heart gallop.

"You're right, mister. It's our fault. We're sorry. We really are." Brandon went on. Desperately trying to stall him until the police arrived.

"It's too late for all that!" Sanderson shouted in an angry outburst. He raised both hands to the side of his head. The blood from his face slid down under his chin. "This wasn't part of my PLAN! I had it all worked out! AND YOU RUINED IT!"

He stretched an arm out and pulled Brandon to him. "If I go down, you're all going with me!" Sanderson threatened. "Night Ghost strikes again!"

Something outside cracked loudly once more. Sanderson turned to the door, guiding the gun with his gaze. As he was distracted, Slim swiftly picked the mace up off the floor and sprayed it into Sanderson's eyes.

"AAAAAAAHHHHHHHHHHH!" he drew back, releasing Brandon and letting the gun clatter to the floor as he hid his face with his hands.

Sanderson grew more frantic. His gravid screaming seemed to fill the entire house. With tear-blurred vision, Sanderson rapidly staggered further off in a befuddled rage. Drops of blood fell to the floor with each step he took.

"Get back here! You can't escape me!"

Suellen and the others watched from where they still stood as Sanderson moved unsteadily towards the open front door. He nearly fell on the flight of stairs, but caught his balance and lurched over to the left, bumping into the side wall before stumbling outside.

"Officer down! Officer down!" the policeman stated through his handheld radio. "Fugitive has vacated the residence. I repeat, the fugitive has vacated the residence."

The blare of police sirens grew louder, obscuring the radio response the officer received. Slim and Brandon bent down to his side.

We need to check on Dad. Suellen thought, still holding her brother close. But dread still swelled in her body like an infection, keeping her from moving. A frail crackle surfaced again from outside, followed by a long splitting rattle. The tearing clatter maintained its crescendo until it came to a clamorous and ripping finish.

Something outside crashed hard into the ground. The impact shook the whole neighborhood like an earthquake. Seized with terror, Suellen dashed to the open doorway and stared out at the cold gray scenery. Sanderson was nowhere in sight. Most of the houses on the other side had long icicles dangling off the gutters.

The tree that stood on the side of the house had now collapsed. Draped with a thick coating of ice, the tree had uprooted from the ground. It now lay in their yard and stretched to the middle of the street.

At the end of the block, several police cars turned onto the street and travelled closer, their sirens blaring all the way. Suellen almost wanted to run outside and wave to get their attention. Just to make sure they didn't pass by. But the authorities continued down and came to a stop in front of the house, their vehicles parked wildly in the street.

Two officers immediately ran over to the fallen tree and stooped down, examining the body of Albert Sanderson who lay unconscious beneath a long branch.

CHAPTER 34

WEDNESDAY AFTERNOON, 1:01 P.M.

The house was now filled with law enforcers. They went from room to room, investigating the premises, collecting evidence, and taking notes.

Suellen, Andre, Slim, and Brandon all sat quietly on the sofa as instructed. Their coats resting behind them across the back of the couch. They watched as two male paramedics carried Officer Thompson away on a stretcher. One of the workers shined a small light in his eyes as they proceeded out the front door.

"Not to worry. He'll be fine," said Police Chief Dawson as he exited the kitchen. Walking on to the center of the room, he stood in front of them and pushed the glasses up on his face. "The bullet mostly hit him in the vest. But he was slightly grazed. And as far as the gas, most of it was spread throughout the kitchen. There wasn't nearly enough in this room to cause an ignition from the gun flare."

"At least he's alright," Slim said, putting on her baby blue trench coat.

Chief Dawson nodded, "That's certainly a good thing. And Suellen, Andre, two of my officers are escorting your grandparents over here as we speak. Paramedics will have your father up here and set to go to the hospital in a few. He suffered a hard strike to the head. But he'll make it. Looks as though he was attacked with the tire iron we discovered in the kitchen.

"We believe that to be the same weapon which brought down the officer who was surveying the area earlier today. He was put in the trunk of his vehicle not far from here. Lost quite a bit of blood. But we found him just in time."

He pulled out a small notepad from his pocket and began to read. "Sabrina Morrison, I've been informed that your mother has been notified and is carpooling here with the mother of Brandon Dowell, who has also been notified."

"Did that guy really do all that just to try to kill us?" Brandon asked with a look of angst.

"I'm afraid so," Chief Dawson replied, putting the notepad back in his pocket. "The window in the laundry room shows signs of forced entry. You kids have to understand that he's a very mentally ill man. As I know you all have already been a witness to."

"I thought he would have killed us all for sure," Andre stated with his head down. "I mean... he just snapped. I've never seen anything like it."

Chief Dawson observed them carefully on the couch, one by one. His mind searched for the right words to put their trauma to rest. "It's difficult to pinpoint why people like him.... are the way they are," he started. "Could be a number of different factors. And you'll drive yourself crazy trying to figure it out. The simplest way I can phrase it, is that when things started not going his way at the end his mind didn't know how to process it. And that made him even more unstable."

"I heard one of the policeman say earlier that he was hiding his vehicle in the forest preserve," said Suellen.

"That's correct," Chief Dawson answered. "He's been altering his hiding grounds from there to the abandoned funeral home. And there's evidence that suggests he's the one who caused the fire there yesterday morning."

Brandon rubbed his forehead and sighed. "I just feel so bad. I can't believe all this happened 'cause of what we did."

"You kids shouldn't feel bad at all," said Dawson with assurance. "What you did was help us catch a very dangerous man without any loss of life. I've got almost thirty years of police work under my belt. And in that time, I can honestly say that I've only had a handful of cases where things transpired like they did here. As far as I'm concerned, that's a pretty strong victory."

"So what happens to him now," Slim asked, wiping tears from her eyes.

"Well," Dawson said through a heavy sigh, "I just got word of his arrival at the hospital. Looks as though all he's got is a fractured leg. And he'll probably need stitches for his jaw. Should know more later. But he's going to be kept there and watched around the clock until we get the okay to have him discharged. He won't be going anywhere without us knowing it. And once he's out, he'll be hit with multiple new charges.

"All of which will follow him on his trip back to Texas where our southern counterparts will have their turn with him. Thanks to you kids, they can now tie him to two other murders there from over three years ago. So I can almost promise you, he will never see the light of day again."

Suellen gazed at the chief and smiled. "That's the best news I've heard all day."

Dawson grinned back at her. "I couldn't agree more, young lady."

From behind them, a female paramedic emerged through the kitchen doorway, pulling Mr. Blanchard along behind her on a stretcher. She was a short, tiny woman with blonde hair tied up in the back. Suellen was surprised the woman could handle carrying her father by herself.

"He's ready, Sir," she said to Chief Dawson. He nodded in response.

Andre was first to stand from the sofa. "Is there anything else we should know?" he asked.

The officer shook his head. "That's everything, I believe. We're going to get all four of you checked out as well. Just to make sure there's no internal damage or anything. And I'll personally inform your relatives of your whereabouts so they can get to you as soon as possible. Now let's get you kids taken care of."

Chief Dawson waited for them to get their belongings. Then he led them around the sofa and to the front door. One of the paramedics from earlier stepped back inside and stood next to the officer.

"Chad, we're all finished here," Dawson said, taking his hat off and scratching the top of his head. "Would you mind taking Sabrina and Brandon on ahead?"

The man turned to them with his short dark hair and heavy sideburns, and smiled. "Not a problem, Sir. You two can come with me."

They waved to their two companions, then followed the man out into the cold midday.

The female paramedic brought Mr. Blanchard over closer and stopped in front of Suellen and Andre. His eyes were barely open, but as he lay there, they saw a slight grin on their father's face.

"Well, there are my two junior crime fighters," he muttered.

Without another word, they clinched their father in a warm hug.

"Careful. He's still in some pain," said the paramedic.

Dawson then stepped over and patted him on the shoulder. "We'll get you back to putting out fires in no time, Chief Blanchard. And I'll get someone in here to clean up this gas."

"I would definitely appreciate it," Charles replied as they let him go.

The paramedic continued pulling Mr. Blanchard on the stretcher while his children walked along beside it. Feeling the harsh frigid air from outside, Suellen zipped her coat up the rest of the way before exiting the house.

Most of their neighbors were already out, standing behind police barriers while talking amongst themselves. Looking over the crowd, Suellen started to feel a bit uncomfortable with so many people around staring at their house. *If they only knew.*

As they neared the ambulance, she spotted Brandon's friend, Derrick Jeffers. Their eyes met. And he waved to her. She cheerfully waved back, then gazed out at the towering hazy clouds as they moved across the sky.

CHAPTER 35

MONDAY AFTERNOON, 3:11 P.M.

A light snow had been falling on a consistent basis all day long. It now covered the grass and sidewalks as Suellen and Andre hurried through the double doors of the school. They stepped outside, eager to get home.

As the two continued walking, other students waiting outside glanced their way. Some were pointing and whispering amongst each other. Despite their parents' wishes to keep matters quiet, word had gotten out that Suellen, Andre, Slim, and Brandon were involved in the capture of a notorious killer. They had been the gossip of the town for a while now. As well as being seen as local heroes.

"No ride home today?" Someone shouted to them.

She and her brother sighed irritably. But neither stopped walking down the wide middle path.

"No, not today," Suellen replied, zipping her pink parka up a little more. "No one was available. So we're back to walking home."

Suellen and Andre met the crossing guard at the curb. She smiled, then limped her way to the streets' center with her stop sign.

"You kids stay safe, now," she said as they passed her.

"We will. Thanks, ma'am," Andre stated.

They continued down the straight path until reaching the next street.

It had been nearly three weeks since their encounter with Albert Sanderson during the ice storm. In that time, the funeral home in the cemetery had been demolished. And the entire sidewalk was now blocked off. So they decided to walk home on the next street over.

As they turned onto the block, Slim and Brandon came running up next to them.

"What is it about catching a serial killer that makes everyone want to be your friend?" Brandon remarked. "Everyone just kept on talking to us in the hallway. Slim and I practically had to pry ourselves out the building."

"Why do you think we left so quick?" Suellen said through laughter. "I guess people suddenly think you're interesting when you've been in both the local and school newspaper. And on television."

As they walked along, the wind blew against them. Slim fastened the last button on her dark blue winter coat that fell to her knees and pulled her hat down over her ears. "Yeah, but that was almost a month ago," she said. "That should be old news by now."

Andre wiped fallen snowflakes off his dark gray coat. "Well, I think it has more to do with that cash reward everyone knows we got last week."

"You can't really blame them, I guess, then," Brandon said. He bent down and scooped up a handful of snow in his bare hand. "Sixty thousand split four ways isn't bad at all. But my mom's not letting me touch a dime until I'm sixteen."

He made a tiny snowball and threw it out, but it blew back against his red pullover coat.

"Smooth move, Brandon," someone shouted from behind them.

They all spun around and saw Derrick Jeffers running towards them in his dark green coat and hat across the snow covered street. He grinned at Suellen as he made his way to the sidewalk. She couldn't help but smile back as he ran up to her.

"Hi, Suellen," he greeted. Clouds of breath flowed from his mouth as he panted. Derrick handed her a notebook he carried in a gloved hand. "You left this under your seat after fifth period today," he said, staring at her through his glasses. "By the time I noticed it you were already gone."

"Thanks." Still smiling, she took her notebook and held it under her arm.

"Heads up," Slim warned before a snowball struck Derrick in his dark, bushy hair. He scooped it out and threw it back at Brandon, hitting him in his chest.

"I'm sorry, D.J.," Brandon chuckled. "But with all that hair I couldn't help myself."

Derrick shook his head and kept smiling. Then he looked back at Suellen and beamed a smile at her.

As they began walking again, Slim, Brandon, and Andre strolled ahead of the group on the shoveled path while Suellen and Derrick followed behind. Suellen kept looking forward, pretending she didn't see him staring at her with his warm eyes.

"Thanks again for finding my notebook," she stated, not knowing what else to say. "I didn't even know I left it."

"I was going to give it to Brandon, but I didn't run into him. And when I saw you all going this way, I ran to catch up."

"I appreciate it." She turned his way. He still had snowflakes in his thick wavy hair.

"So how's your father doing?" Derrick asked genuinely.

"He's much better now," she replied, stroking her hair with a gloved hand. "He was only in the hospital a day and a half. And the next day he was back at work. Ever since my mom came back she's been trying to convince him to take a week off to recuperate. And every week he says he will but never does."

She watched Derrick laugh, staring at the dark skin that made up his young handsome face.

"Well, that's still good," he said. "And I hear that guy got sent back to Texas. So that's *really* good."

Suellen nodded. "Two days ago. The police called early Saturday morning and told us."

"Wow, that was crazy. When I heard that tree fall, I didn't know what had happened. But I never would have imagined all that was going on."

"Yeah it was," she said. "We're just glad it's all over, though."

"So am I. But I'm glad you all are alright. Wouldn't want anything to happen to you. I'd be heartbroken."

Through the corner of her eye, Suellen saw Derrick continue to gaze at her with a wide grin, admiring her. She couldn't help but giggle. But Suellen was still rather distraught. At times when she was alone she found herself checking over her shoulder, half expecting Sanderson to be there, stalking her.

They had all talked the situation over with their parents. Everything seemed to be fine for her friends and Andre. Suellen felt as though she was the only one unable to move past it. Until now as she walked alongside Derrick.

"There it is, crew," said Brandon. "Nothing but a huge pile of bricks and wood now."

They all turned and stared over the ditch to the former building that once stood above the hill. There were police barriers around the pile and a large green dumpster had been placed on the sidewalk.

"It's about time," Slim said as they continued on.

"They couldn't tear that place down fast enough for me," Andre remarked.

But Suellen felt a sense of caution. She somehow felt threatened by the site. She couldn't turn away from the snowy ditch. Some of the trees below had lost limbs and branches during the ice storm. The ones that remained were blanketed with a small portion of snow. The dry dead leaves that hid the dull grass were also covered in white.

It's over, Suellen scolded herself. *I can't let this thing bother me the rest of my life. He's not there. He's in Texas now where he'll spend the rest of his life behind bars. So don't start looking for things that aren't there.*

"You okay, Suellen?" Derrick asked. He reached an arm to her shoulder as his eyes squinted with concern.

Suellen steered her gaze away from the ditch, putting her morbid feelings to rest. "I am now." A cold breeze arose, gently blowing her hair as falling snow flew at her face.

"That's good to know," said Derrick, smiling again.

She gently grabbed Derrick by his wrist and guided him away from the steep trench as they caught up with the group.

They moved past the old cemetery and crossed over onto the next block without looking back.

About the Author

Nicholas Christopher Brady was born in Chicago, Illinois and grew up in Northwest Indiana. Since an early age, he has loved reading books by R.L. Stine, James Baldwin, Christopher Paul Curtis, Mildred Taylor , and many others. It was his love for reading that helped hone his skills and gradually manifested into a passion for writing.

By the time he was 13, he had already started writing his first book *Danger in the House*, which was published shortly after he graduated high school. And a year later, he released his second title, *Strangers in the Swamp*. Nick's writing style has been described as highly engaging and keeps readers hooked to the storyline. As described by fellow author John Darryl Winston, "Brady does a phenomenal job of combining action, dialogue, and description, the sign of a skilled writer." Readers can easily relate to his diverse characters that drive the story page after page. And although he depicts his target audience as young adults, adults enjoy his unique stories as well.

Nick's latest thriller, *Night Ghost* first came to him during his senior year in high school. But he didn't start officially writing it until years later while he attended college at Purdue University. After earning his Bachelors in English/Writing, Nick began working with children first as a Tutor/Mentor then as a Reading Interventionist. He plans to eventually become a college instructor in creative writing. In addition to writing, Nick enjoys listening to music, traveling, and spending time with family and friends.

AUTHOR'S NOTE

      First and foremost, I want to say that I appreciate you taking the time to read *Night Ghost*, my friends. Be on the look out for more thrillers coming out in the future!
      One of my main goals as a writer is to entertain and keep audiences intrigued in the world I create from the beginning to the end. If you feel I accomplished that then I would be grateful if you took a moment of your time to write a review on Amazon for *Night Ghost*. I feel reviews are a helpful method to gain more insight from satisfied readers.
      Thank you, and it's an honor to have you as a reader. And for those who have been asking me, yes there will be a sequel to *Night Ghost*. Albert Sanderson isn't finished yet, not by a long shot!